ADAM'S BIG BANG

Other Titles in the Adam Quatrology

The Electroencephalographer Couldn't Cry
Return of the Horla
The Radio

ADAM'S BIG BANG

A NOVEL

BERNARD SUSSMAN

Bartleby Press
Washington • Baltimore

Copyright © 2012, 2019 by Bernard Sussman

Cover design by Ross Feldner
Illustration by Bernard Shleien

ISBN 978-0935437-54-6
Library of Congress Control Number: 2011940645

Published by:

Bartleby Press

PO Box 858
Savage, Maryland 20763
800-953-9929
www.BartlebythePublisher.com

Printed in the United States of America

To Alexandra MacMaster

One

A calamitous prediction.

"...And nothing would be left, not even memory."

Only rounding a corner and running smack into God would be more extraordinary and yet this barely lesser revelation was being tossed off so casually by a confident voice.

It was a late night radio interview of a Harvard physicist who had little else to say. Adam, at first barely picking up on any of it, had been sitting at the kitchen table, rather more interested in what his dogs were up to than what this radio chatter might be all about. But slowly, the physicist's pronouncement, with most of its cosmological implications, was beginning to get to him

Oddly enough, this astounding bit of aired commentary would fail to draw even the slightest reaction from the press. Nor would it be picked up on by the general radio audience either. No more, it would seem, than by his dogs. They remained at their usual stations for that time of night, the Doberman erect, staring up at him intently and demandingly, her concerns fixed solely on the merest possibility of still another biscuit to devour; the wolfhound sprawled inertly, disjointedly, jaw pressed against the floor, but occasionally raising one or other brow as if in expectation of something about to happen. Unbeknownst to him, it had already. That is if one considers the total revision of one man's essential orientation, a happening.

The radio program was mere superficial media fluff sparked by a new astronomical observation appearing to confirm, at long last, apparently once and for all, that the big bang theory was truly the way everything had come about. It was not any interest in that remote beginning which managed to divert Adam's attention from his beloved dogs. It was what now, all of a sudden, was so obviously predictable by way of a universal ending. In fact, if one accepted that dreadful finality, one would be hard put to harbor any lingering fascination for whatever had moved the beginning.

For what the prominent Harvard physicist had said, and all too matter of factly, was quite startling. Based upon recent findings that proved the big bang theory, the heavenly bodies were set upon a diverging course and racing apart at great velocity. Nothing much new in that. What was new, however, was the now generally accepted conviction that eventually all of those stars and planets must at some point in the future lose their forward momentum, decelerate, stall, and fall back in reverse direction colliding with one another. Consequently, all matter would converge to form a small sphere of infinite density and because of this enormous compaction there'd follow an utterly destructive explosion, another big bang, and the shaping of new emergences.

What might come of such a cataclysm and fresh start, by way of life forms or anything else, was to the Harvard fellow's mind unpredictable, save for a singular certainty.

He reasoned that since everything existing must disappear in that blast which would take all matter back down to atomic and subatomic particles, so also would every man-made mechanism affirming his existence. There could not survive, he argued, any sort of inscription, space drifting capsule with encoded messages, tapes, hard drives, computer chips. Nothing would endure.

And if, by the remotest possibility, some kind of intelligence did eventually evolve from out a new primordium, there'd be no way for it to know what had gone before. For the thing we call memory, it would be a complete wipeout.

Well so what? Why should Adam care about a catastrophe slated to come bearing down on us in a billion years or more? He'd be long gone by then. That was for sure. And anyway, hadn't certain religions even foretold such eternal recurrent goings and comings? Big bang restructurings might very well be the integral pattern for an order of things somehow ordained.

All the same, Adam became increasingly uneasy, finding no comfort by the recollection of what he ordinarily regarded as so much crack pot religious mumbo jumbo, however much it fell in line with new wave science. In fact he'd prefer to be as ignorant about all of this as his dogs. At his time of life he could do without the disequilibrium of any confounding new revelations. Things were all right just the way they were. In short order he found himself wishing that this particular disclosure could be made to go away.

For that reason, in spite of the lateness of the hour, he found himself hard-pressed to sift this matter through, maybe even get it behind him. Past midnight or not, he'd stay up a while longer. Going to bed was out of the question. For what? Just to lie awake, anguished by the question of why it should be that after so many millions of years, all of this had to be happening now, to him, in his time? After all, he'd turned sixty-six. It wouldn't have been too much longer for him to pass on in a state of blissful ignorance of this impending disaster, peculiarly comforted by his heretofore prevailing notion that whatever the eventual fate of the ground under him, there had to be at least some kind of stability out there in the cosmos. Sure, planets might come and go, but who'd imagine them all vaporizing at once, in a flash, with the possibility of any kind of communication or record keeping going up in smoke at the same time? And nothing to be left to communicate with or about?

Adam, whether or not he'd spoken of it, had nurtured the idea, which he found comforting, that every human move, even his own puny ones, could always manage to be somehow recorded and memorialized. He was prompted to recall that his mother had sometimes cautioned him, "Remember, Adam. Nothing is forever." But she'd only meant that things didn't last. She'd had no idea that forever, even the mere concept of it, was to be up for grabs.

A short time later, as was his custom, Adam led the dogs outside to relieve themselves. Then, having given up on the prospect of anything more to eat, they ambled disinterestedly towards other rooms in his old house to settle down for the night. It was not the best time of day for his sixty-six-year-old brain to be speculating or attempting to unravel monumental scientific propositions, but because it needed to be done, how to begin?

Music might help. Adam had always found that recorded music stirred him, sometimes even managing his transport into inspirational dimensions often attended by colorful visual aberrations. Not loudly though, this time, or he'd disturb his wife, who was by then asleep in the room above. Bach sprang instantly to mind as the clear choice. He started up a recently acquired recording of the Toccata and Fugue, performed on the great organ of a Dresden cathedral. With the first pedal notes, however, he sensed, unfortunately, that extreme loudness was indispensable to his needs. To that end he switched off briefly then resumed his listening, but over headphones, so as not to awaken his wife.

There had often been moments like this when Adam would set his mind adrift under the influence of a favored musical selection. Unusual imagery was apt to appear or a novel idea take form. On occasion, such experiences had managed to change his way of thinking or to effect a turn in his day to day affairs.

But nothing of that sort was happening now. The truth was, and Adam didn't know it, but he might never have another musically induced brain storm. Not because this particular music was failing to affect him. It was, and to an exaggerated degree. But the sad part of his present situation was that the music, although no longer thought provoking, was indeed transparently beautiful, exquisitely moving, even perfect. There was not the possibility of it being excelled. In fact, this was the first time he could really enjoy the Toccata in that kind of way, a sensual one. But an odd new mental drift had taken hold of him obliging a response to the import of all sound, all music, this or any other Bach composition, as well as everything else, being utterly doomed.

With the future now astonishingly finite and fragile, paradoxically, the present had been made barren, however delicious it might seem for the moment. But if extremities of sensation were only to be rooted in the ephemeral, Adam wondered what if anything, might be left to give him sustained satisfaction.

Certainly more customary kinds of detachment, those cultivated to foster the lesser fulfillments of a creative bent of mind, were hardly still appealing. They were quite pointless, anyway, in this newly limited universe. To bother about evolving anything, including the powers of his mind, made absolutely no sense in the new found reality of the impending galactic blind alley.

That is how Adam, at sixty-six, a newly retired surgeon, who'd been casting about for productive ways to spend the rest of his life, began for the first time to see his situation in a completely different light. No longer was he apt to dwell on what had been important to him in the past or even on what might seem promising about the future. For how could anything, be it of the past or future, be regarded as having significance? Nor was there a conceivable point in trying to make distinctions between them.

In the end, would it not be all the same? Was a world, a man, a man's works, his own works, any more important than were his dogs, or for that matter a single one of their fleas? Everything was headed for the same oblivion. Was it not? It had even become reasonable to suggest that only atoms or quarks were privileged with significance, for they at least had a claim on immortality and could forever rearrange the shape of things to come.

A brief radio program had moved Adam to give up on work and on life as he had always taken them and to end his day wondering what might possibly be contrived to afford him pleasure.

Two

Adam was still in bed at eleven. Clare was downstairs making coffee and talking to the dogs. Such smells and sounds found easy updraft access to second floor rooms in their old stone house.

It had been home to them for more than thirty years but started out rather as a barn as far back as 1809. Assembled from big rocks barged down to Washington over the Chesapeake and Ohio Canal or stones quarried from the banks of neighboring streams, it had been mortared together by the skilled craftsmen of that time. The original structure was added onto and converted to living quarters in the mid-thirties, but so primitively that their time worn residence was victim to monumental drafts and occasional leakage from both rain and ground water.

Now, even after more than 65 years of innovatively engineered improvements, it could still admit the occasional odor of automotive exhaust from adjacent streets. On rainy days of particularly heavy downpour, these might find admixture with foul emanations from nearby sewers, along with swamp gases out of prehistoric wet places

"Don't joke about it. I'm sick, and being sick is a full-time job, that's if you're going to be any good at it, it is."

"You are not sick. You're just bored silly. You need something to do. Hanging around here all day and moping is not the answer."

"Look, cutting open somebody's heart isn't the absolute end all."

And certainly not now it wasn't. Not since last night when he'd learned precisely just what the absolute end all stood to be.

"It sure was for you. I warned you not to quit. You're always so damned impulsive, and then you wind up with these god awful second thoughts and can't stop torturing yourself. Maybe you could still go back. How's that for an idea? Why don't you go in and have a nice little talk with the dean?"

"Forget it. I'm through with all of those bastards. You got anything else to bug me with, or are you just here to see if I'm still alive?"

"Only that Oscar is downstairs."

"Oscar? Are you kidding? Now? Here? This early?"

"Adam, it's past eleven."

"What's he doing?"

"What he always does. Staring out the window, humming a little, joking around, chuckling at something up there in his head, and every once and awhile he stops and scribbles in that same old beat-up pad he's always got with him. I suppose there's another song in the works."

"He's not entering it into my computer, is he? Last week I tried to bring up angioplasty and got a damned musical lament for some kind of a black bitch."

"No, Adam. But the poor man has been hanging around

down there and patiently waiting for you to get out of bed for over an hour. So come on. Move along. It must be about something important. And what if he does type one of his neat little songs into that creaky old computer of yours? You keep saying you've given up on being a doctor. If you really mean it, why not let that dumb machine of yours have a little fun. No?"

"Look, tell him I'll be down in a couple of minutes. Just let me grab a quick shower."

Adam knew only too well what Oscar Brown Jr., his old show biz friend, was there for. It had to be in line with an understanding they'd reached only the week before, a commitment on Adam's part, which given his new state of mind, might no longer be possible to hold to.

With little else these days to occupy him, Adam had agreed, of all things, to write Oscar's life story. It had come down to a choice between that or having to hear a lot more of what had become Oscar's incessant nagging for Adam to be his personal agent. Something "drastic" was urgently called for, according to Oscar, if he was ever going to "cash in" during the years remaining to him. He was in desperate need of being "promoted."

Of course, Adam had neither the experience nor the taste for traveling around the country trying to inveigle night club owners, colleges, or theatrical producers into bookings for his friend, which is what Oscar had really wanted. So, instead of that, Adam had come up with his own idea, that of writing a kind of biography. Oscar, after due consideration, seemed to catch onto the idea, even thinking it a not half-bad ploy. Their joint reasoning was that if such a book did manage to sell, or even if it only drew a certain amount of attention, well, so would Oscar Brown Jr.

The problem was that Adam had never tried his hand at biography. His only writing had been on medical subjects. Nevertheless, he was willing to have a go at it. He was for anything, short of becoming some kind of a show business agent, if it might advance this remarkable fellow's career. God knows, to his mind it had been an incredible oversight or flaw in some obscure order of things for Oscar, like himself, to have turned sixty-five but having managed neither his well-deserved share of fame, nor any fortune that Adam was aware of. He could certainly think of no one else in show business with Oscar's measure of talent. Oscar was unique.

This morning, what Oscar must surely have come for was to hand over the chronology of his life and musical career. It was intended to serve as the bare bones outline for the biography to come. To come, of course, from Adam.

In the shower, Adam recalled how startled then amused his friend had been over his initial suggestion that perhaps the book might even be written about an Oscar freshly expired but still unlucky enough to have passed on without ever having become popular.

Adam had proposed that the first chapter start out with Adam being interviewed by some kind of investigative reporter seeking inside information about the now dead but belatedly appreciated entertainer, a fellow scarcely known anymore save for some dozen old recordings or published songs, and barely recalled stage shows and night club engagements. And Adam would put it to the reporter right then and there. He'd come up with some jottings of what he proposed and read them to Oscar the week before.

"You know, I always used to wonder if some day this would happen. That a guy like you would come out of nowhere, walk in here and ask 'What was he really like?' Isn't it pathetic that now, and it's not too long after he died, that people are finally talking him up and catching on to his having been a musical and poetic genius? And all of a sudden there's all this curiosity about who he actually was. I suppose you know that when he died he hadn't had a recording contract or cut a record on his own in more than twenty years? And that's what you get for being a genius? Or at least that's what this particular black genius, who never once failed to be spectacular, or to move his audience, got for all of his trying.

"And now, just so you can maybe write him up a little better, I'm supposed to answer your questions? Mister, I don't really see the point in it. He's gone. Oscar's gone. He's all gone now and none of his old friends, or his kids, or those who got such a kick out of hearing him, need you to tell them how great he was. They know it all too well. They knew it the first time they heard him sing. And they're not going to know it any better than they do right now for what you, a complete stranger, might get it in your head to write. All they'd be thinking, and wondering, and asking themselves over and over, would be where in hell were guys like you when he was here, when he was alive, trying to make it, when he could have used you?

"But I'll do it. I'll do it anyway, for old time's sake and because that's how I'll get to remember Oscar once again. I'd like that. Not that it can do him any good now, the poor dead bastard. That's the terrible sad truth and the shame of it all. Oscar's dead and the time for helping him has past. It's over. Over."

And then, after the reading, Oscar and Adam had sat silently together, awed both by Oscar's prefigured demise and the prospect of actually getting something that commanding into print. Until Oscar, with a grunt, his blue eyes enlivened, broke the spell.

"Uh. That's something else. But maybe just a tad too premature. Damn. It's enough to scare the livin' shit outa me. So how about draftin' somethin' maybe a little different for the first chapter?"

Christ. Adam wondered as he toweled off, what was he to do now? Now that he found himself with no taste for any kind of workaday endeavor? How could his agreement to promote Oscar's career hold up, given his new attitude? Oscar would hardly take kindly to the idea that just because universal collapse was in the offing, neither he nor his songs counted for very much.

Adam was caught in an unforeseen dilemma. How could he possibly go downstairs and square any of this with his old friend? Tell him that their deal was off, that he intended to let him down simply because, as far as he was concerned, their understanding lacked ultimate meaning. That no one gets to make their mark in a world headed for oblivion and expect something like that to play out amicably?

It was more than reluctance to be an instrument of betrayal that had him apprehensive. Once Oscar got started on anything at all he was a veritable dynamo. He developed an irresistible momentum. It was surely inconceivable that in the matter of how his professional career might be turned around during these, his "last chance" years, Oscar would do anything but burn to get on with it. Ever since

Adam had agreed to mastermind and implement Oscar's overdue ascendancy, a fire had already been well stoked. So how could this whole enterprise be anything but unstoppably energized?

Energy. Unstoppable energy. Everything connected with Oscar had lots of that. Adam could never forget how, thirty-five years before, it had burst upon him.

It was eleven-thirty at night and he'd been in his bedroom looking finally to get some sleep. The day had been spent in surgery and examining patients. Beyond being tired, Adam was feeling that his life had turned monotonous and worse, tedious.

Up to that moment he had no knowledge, much less experience of monkeys, or anything else, which did a thing called "signify." His only purpose in turning on the radio had been to catch the late night weather forecast. But that's not what he got. What he got was enough to always remember, for it being everlastingly flashed in his memory as a programmed association, the precise arrangement of everything in that bedroom. Adam could scarcely recall the contents of any other room in that house, much less the general layout, but he would never forget that bedroom. It's where he was put on to Oscar and a thing called "signifyin'."

Suddenly, from out the radio, there was this astounding voice. What point in trying to describe it further? How, he always thought, might mere characterization ever manage to do the essence of that voice full justice? To his mind there were enormous limitations placed upon mere words in matters of musical taste and people should eschew the commonly invoked banalities like "terrific" or "awesome" and so many other exclamatory or visceral ways to describe oneself as being moved. Nor did more erudite, finer tuned, acclamations ever fill the bill, either.

He settled, at the time, for certitude that this voice was different. It stood apart. It was overwhelmingly funny, commandeered your attention. You'd recognize it again instantly, anywhere. It grabbed hold of your mood, displacing whatever else might be there, and hurried you along with it, captive to its rollicking and insistent rhythm.

Adam, a man of conservative, self-disciplined ways, someone who'd be called a "square," always remembered later how he'd sat on the edge of his bed, transfixed, straining not to miss a single note or word of what was being musically represented somewhere, out there, in an old-time jungle.

It was in such a place, according to this voice, the voice of Oscar Brown Jr., that a monkey of the "signifyin'" kind had conspired to arrange for varied sorts of whippin' of an unfriendly lion by an elephant provoked by that same monkey to deliver his very painful message to the effect that lions, subsequently harboring an eternal grudge over the matter, and also thereby considering all monkeys to be accountable, held them in obligation of "stayin' up in them trees...to this very day."

Well, this was not something to just be mulled over. Adam had been made so restless, so captive to the musical beat, and so humored by the ludicrous nature of this tall tale, which he would later learn Oscar had toned down considerably out of obscenity considerations, that he was swept away.

Before the lyrics could be repeated he was impelled to awaken Clare that she might share in his marveling over this madcap musical explosion. Quickly captivated also, she was forthwith of a similar mind regarding the merit of Mr. Oscar Brown Jr.

Tired as Adam was that night, it was hard getting off to sleep. He kept hearing that damned "Signifyin' Monkey" number, was even driven to humming it to himself. It just couldn't be turned off. From then on nothing was the same. Oscar had entered his life and for the next thirty-five years he'd always be there signifyin' (that is, inciting or stirring up) something or other. And all of that without yet seeing Oscar in the flesh. That would come later.

The next day, refrains of "Signifyin' Monkey" recurred. There were moments at times with patients, and even during surgery, that he was compelled to consider such intrusions brazenly inappropriate, if not offending of the serious and demanding nature of his work.

Undeterred, however, by such uppity notions, the stubbornly catchy words and music held their ground. In fact it was so relentless that Adam began to wonder if once a thing--be it words or music or ideas, or as in this case a simple little ditty--intruded or latched on to a pathway in a person's nervous system, it was really feasible by sheer exercise of will to drive it back out. Or rather, under special circumstances, and God forbid this be one of them, it might take parasitic hold of a person's brain, appropriate its own groovy reverberating circuit, and like certain old time popular music, just keep going "round and round."

This unfolding fascination with Oscar's voice and the "Signifyin' Monkey" number, along with musings on their odd appeal, inclined Adam at the time to actually speculate if there was not some kind of physiological linkage between such an obsession and the phenomenon of the ideé fixé, unrelenting paranoid delusions, and the like of similar intransigent psychological habitudes.

With both Oscar and the "Signifyin' Monkey" number having such a grip on him, cycling over and over again in his ears, and in his brain, there were times he questioned, with real anxiety, if all of this would ever quit. What a fate, to have one's mind taken over by a musical virus.

But that was long ago. Adam, quite moved now by these remembrances of how it had all begun, started down the stairs How could he possibly do anything to disappoint his friend? How, conceivably, might one let such a fellow down?

Three

Oscar was solicitous.

"How you doin'?"

"Not bad. But feeling our age and I need to stop this sleeping late business. It can lead to all kinds of trouble, like strokes and coronaries. Take your pick. We old timers need to keep everything moving. Stasis has a way of knocking us off."

"Uhh, uhh."

Oscar tended to be awed by Adam's medical pronouncements. Particularly those concerning the aging process, now that he had also turned the corner on sixty-five.

"Well, if that's how it is, I'm gonna damned well live forever. Movin's my special thing. How's about that. I'm on to the very elixir of life."

He'd hit it right on the on the head. Oscar lived the life of a restless, reveling, showman, a gypsy of sorts, rarely settling down in any one place for more than a day or two. And Adam was well aware that during his brief stopovers, he rarely slept like most people.

Oscar had a way of coming awake every few hours,

getting up to complete the phrasing of some lyric, then writing it down, or fashioning a line of melody if only to store it by a mysterious method he had for remembering them. With no formal musical education, and never having learned musical notation, he'd always had to do it like that, by ear and memory.

As for sitting still, it was utterly foreign to him. Always squirming, twisting, gesturing, he was ever "on." Except for those occasional other moments when, all of a sudden, he'd seem to go blank, and drop off into one of his cat naps. Adam had the idea that such brief interludes played a critical role in sustaining him.

There followed some more of their usual banter, leading eventually, as both might well expect from past experience, to a stand off over uncompromising differences of opinion.

"No such luck, Oscar."

"What you sayin?"

"Living forever. You said you had the elixir for it."

"Well I was only kiddin'. An' I don't really want to live forever. All I want is what I'm best at for as long as I can, and to help my kids, and just dig it."

"Really? Well I would like to live forever. And you want to know something? When I say it, I'm only serious."

Adam was trying to bait his friend. He'd drawn the line: "I'm only serious", from another of Oscar's songs, one he was particularly proud of and often performed. But Oscar let it pass if only to take a dismissive tack with him.

"Hell, Adam. Even if you could live forever, you wouldn't know what to do with all a' that time."

"Listen, man. If I had it, I'd do myself proud spending

every second of it. Even knowing it'd have no end, I'd still play each moment like it stood to be the very last."

Oscar snickered derisively acting as if he knew Adam too well to buy any of that. Then he turned reflective.

"Adam, I do not understand why you are always carryin' on the way you do. Why not simply take life as you find it? You come. You do what you can. You give it your best shot. You go. That's it. That's all there is. Period. Anything more is bullshit. An' you can't get anything more because there's nothing else for the takin'. So be cool, brother, be cool."

"I see. You come. You go. That's easy enough to understand, even for a dumb old saw bones like me. But where in hell you goin' to and comin' from?"

"Not important. All I have to know is that whatever it was that got me here is also set to get me out just fine. It's been fixed. You can make bet on it. An' there's not a damned thing to doubt or to chew over. So just lean back and dig it."

Adam decided to lay the whole thing on him.

"Suppose you had reliable indications that nobody was going anywhere?"

"What you drivin' at now?"

"And that everything, the whole kit and caboodle, including what you've just been scribbling away at in that little song book of yours, is slated to become no more than atomic dust. Not only right down here where we are, but throughout the whole damned universe."

"So? What else is new?"

It was as if Oscar had always been privy to this erstwhile well-kept cosmological secret.

"It doesn't bother you?"

Adam figured his doomsday theme wasn't getting across, and needed to be enlarged upon, so he proceeded to describe in detail what had happened the night before. Assuming he'd rendered his account solemnly enough to invite, at the very least, a respectful amount of countering quiet reflection on Oscar's part, he paused in expectation. But Oscar wasn't thinking it over. His response came fast on the heels of what he'd heard.

"Maybe the problem is in your bein' Jewish. This here nigger ain't got either the time or the inclination for all that fancy soul searchin' or philosophizin' you people are always goin' through. The only thing I need to know is that what I've got at this particular minute is nowhere close to suitin' me, but I'm onto what I need and I've a pretty good idea of where it's at. So screw everything else, especially some dumb thing like where we're all headin' a billion years or more down the road. I couldn't care less. All you and I have to work on is how to get us where we need to be, like tomorrow, man. And Adam. It ain't no shepherd I'm needin' to take me to some promised land or tell me what to want. I damned well know what I want. Now, you gonna help out, like we agreed, or you intendin' to cop out?"

It was also Oscar's moment to wave an envelope under Adam's nose. Adam knew full well what it contained, but enquired anyway.

"What's this?"

"Nothin' much. Just an outline of my life. Remember? You're supposed to start writin' up my story."

"You got right on it, didn't you?"

"Yeah, man. Seize the moment."

"It can't be done."

"What?"

"Catch a moment. And seize it. There is no present; There's just a moving instant, once in awhile, conveying some all too brief pleasure or just as likely, a bit of pain. Reach for the present, and soon you realize it's slipped away, evaporated. There's only the future and the past, but their fate has been decided as well. They're doomed."

"Brother, spare me any more of your intellectual crack of doom baloney. I can tell you that right now, at this very moment, I damned sure very much presently am. And except as maybe I owe somethin' to the idea of what me and my kind have been put through over the years, it bein' my decided purpose to carry on with what I feel needs doin' to sort that out, you and I should just be fo-cusin' on the future, my particular future. We don't have time to spend on anything else. Look here, what's with you, Adam? You're actin' real peculiar. Don't you want to work on our book? You duckin' me? Christ. The whole thing was your damned idea."

"Oscar, believe me. I'd like to do it. It's only that I've been unhinged by that radio program. It's got me doubting the point in doing anything. It's a very weird situation and yet, what I've started to notice is that getting melancholic over everything being so all time ephemeral doesn't actu-ally feel all that bad. I think that maybe it's even got a way of turning me on."

"So that's it?"

"I'm afraid so."

Oscar turned pensive for quite a while, then took a crack at persuasion.

"Well, why don't we look at it like this? The way I'm gettin' it is you figure it's goin' to be tough havin' your kicks like before because now you think you're only turnin' on to what's either slippin' away or standin' to be phased out. You're into what's just about kaput. Right?"

"You make it sound like I've got some kind of a wacko perversion."

"No sir. Not at all. Anytime you wanta do your own thing, it's A-okay with me. It just seems, when you start thinkin' about it, that this here nigger and a book about him fits your new ticket perfectly."

"How'd you come to that?"

"Because Adam, you crazy mother fucker, the commercial side of my career is dead in the water. It is at rock bottom. And there isn't any chance of you gettin' better highs by cozyin' up to anything standin' more to be done for right now than me and my bank account. There just isn't any such thing out there. Anywhere. In or out of that nutty cosmos of yours, there's nothing more defunct at the present time than my black ass and my assets. You beginnin' to get it?"

"And if we pull it off? Write the book?"

"Man, how can you ask such a dumb question? Haven't we been through all a' that? Didn't you yourself call it? You forget how if the book is any kind of a seller, people are gonna' be talkin' me up and writin' me up, and wantin' to see me and hear me? It'll be like bookings, recordings, music videos, talk show spots, maybe even movie deals. The guys who run things couldn't afford to keep ignorin' me."

"So?"

"So? You really have lost it. Do I need to spell that out, too? It's about dough man, all about dough, which right now I do not have any of. And dough, Adam, in case you don't happen to fully appreciate it, is power, and power is bein' able to put on my own shows, trot my own stuff, so I can sit home once in awhile with my feet up and watch big screen TV. And it's bein' able to spend some change on my kids and bring us all together, just for once, in a single neat place, so we can do creative things together. I'd like to have them all around me until my time is up. We wouldn't have to be scattered all over the place like we are now. There's also," he said, winking a blue eye, "a few other cool things that hardly need tellin'."

"Go on. Do it anyway."

"Hell man, foxes. There's foxes, lots of foxes. And gettin' high."

"Seems to me there's no shortage of that right now. Hell. Just last week you were complaining every female agent coming your way winds up in the sack with you instead of tending to business. And how about all that stuff about feeling awkward when one of those gals turns out to be younger than your own daughter?"

"Ever hear about the spice of life, Adam? And you any idea about how much spicy variety money can buy? I gotta hand it to you though. You remember just about everything you hear, don't you? Includin' certain things I'd just as soon you didn't. On balance though, when you think about it, that doggone memory of yours can just about fill the bill right now. That's if you take these notes," he said, stabbing Adam in the chest with his envelope, "and what all else you've got stashed away up there in your head, and get down to doin' some heavy writin'. When you gonna start?"

"The next day or so," Adam conceded, collapsing under Oscar's insistence.

"What you waitin' for, inspiration? Start today. Hell, man, I could die tomorrow. Or the book could hit it big with me havin' one of those strokes you were talkin' about and bein' laid up in some damn nursin' home. Now is the time. Now is our time. While I can still sing and move. Hell, you wanna know somethin' else? My voice is as good, maybe even better than it ever was. It's a damned shame, Adam. I should be out there singin', makin' records, and doin' concerts two, three times a week. We've got no fuckin' time to waste."

"It's not a question of inspiration. It's a mood thing. Maybe after you leave I'll play some of your old records and those tapes I made years ago. That might get me going. I probably just need to stir up some memories."

"Better yet."

"What's that?"

"Come on down to the Barry Theater tonight. I'm doin' a benefit performance. It's as close to a real gig as I can come up with these days. My old records are okay. but I'd rather have you where it's really at, sittin' up front and feelin' it, smellin' it, bein' there. And hell, Man. Maybe also gettin' to appreciate what it is I need to be doin', what I been missin' out on."

"All right. I'll be there."

"There's two shows. Come for the second one. I'll be limbered up by then. Gettin' a little stiff lately 'til I'm warmed up. Arthritis, you think? By now you must know all about that too. Right, old buddy?"

"You mean personally, or as a doctor?"

"Forget it, man. Just forget I said anything. You sure have a funny kinda head. Trouble is, right now it's the only one I've got workin' for me. Just remember to be there. I want you in that front row around nine. Okay? I'm takin' off. Gotta rehearse the piano player."

Oscar rose to leave.

"I'll be there. You can count on it."

Once again Oscar had managed to be energizing. And he didn't really have to ask or make demands upon him. Mere suggestions were usually enough to get Adam going. They "rilly" were.

Four

A dam hadn't been forthcoming. What difference did it make, whether or not Oscar Brown Jr. "made it"? And even if he crafted a well-written account of his life, it could not endure any longer than his own articles labored over so diligently.

It hurt to consider that certain well-regarded scientific papers of his, published finally in prestigious medical journals were headed for cosmic incineration. Everything was slated to go, to turn to cinders, along with anyone hanging around even remotely interested. "Dust to dust" was a pretty good call.

But why just sit around and stew over it? Perhaps, in the same way those unanticipated radio waves of the night before had been so unsettling, he might undergo a countering kind of mental deflection from whatever chance happenstance stood to come of going down to the Barry Theater.

On the other hand there was the abiding question of how to get on with the quest for whatever good feelings might still be mustered in a doomsday environment.

He'd drawn a blank, but it might not be unreasonable to think that from out the milieu of one of his old friend's customarily raucous and rhythmic performances, or the unpredictable and motley kind of crowd Oscar usually drew upon, some sort of lead might materialize. It looked like a fomentation was in order and Oscar, once on stage, could always be counted on to stir things up.

Adam had pause to recall how, a month after hearing Oscar on the radio, he'd been drawn, for the first time, to catch Oscar in live performance at the Gate in Greenwich Village. Odd, was it not, the way both of these unique and tumultuous disturbances of his psychic equilibrium had emanated from air waves?

But so dissimilar were those commotions. From the very outset, Oscar's fervent cajoling voice projected vitality and extended a ribald warm hearted summons to good natured celebration. By contrast, the icy pronouncement of the previous night's program constituted a coldly indifferent consignment to oblivion in a non-caring void.

To put that chilling business out of mind Adam focussed on recalling that adventurous long past evening at the Village Gate.

How lucky he'd thought himself to find a front row seat because Oscar had a packed house. Then, almost upon ordering his drink, right up there on the stage immediately above him and appearing to smile down upon him alone, was this droll, twisting and grinning, black man. The little guy had blue eyes and they were alive with a mischievous taunting energy.

Adam became more and more intrigued as in easy sequence, first came "Signifyin' Monkey" and then so many other crowd pleasers. Applause and screams reverberated through the room each time Oscar completed a number. If the audience had had its rowdy insistence Oscar would never have managed to finish that first set and gotten off the stage.

For Adam, there was no choice but to stay for the second show. It was also inevitable that he would slip back-stage afterwards and line up with other well wishers at Oscar's dressing room door.

There was a handsome, young black woman there, who mistaking Adam for some kind of a theatrical type, introduced herself as "Mister Brown's protégée." Adam was barely able to follow her misdirected pitch at self-promotion eager as he was to keep his place in the line inching its way in Oscar's direction.

Finally, when he and Oscar did come face to face, he hurried through a description of how he'd happened to hear the fateful broadcast of "Signifyin' Monkey" and of how much he'd enjoyed the night's performance. These two opposites somehow locked onto one another, and an understanding, not ever to be defined, was struck.

Adam, who had never before had such a reaction, nor felt impelled to even approach a performer, much less seek one out backstage, was captivated. Oscar, who had all manner of peculiar people turning up at performances, as well as elsewhere in his frenetic life, seemed nevertheless curious about Adam. They exchanged telephone numbers and parted, Oscar with the beautiful black woman in tow, Adam on his own to get back to Clare and excitedly describe his thrilling evening in the Village. It appeared that a relationship had begun.

Adam decided to ready himself for the evening at the Barry Theater by playing a few of Oscar's old vinyl recordings. He settled down in the den and drew one album from the shelf on which several were stacked.

The record jacket was depressingly dusty. It featured, to one side of the cover, the face of a very youthful appearing Oscar, eyes soulfully closed, apparently in song. That record had become an RCA collectors' series item, and was also Oscar's only recording still available in the United States. Over on the right side of the jacket there were commentaries:

Bob Arnold: "Producing radio programs for eight years, I have heard many neophytes from stage and screen. There's no one who has bowled me over like Oscar Brown Jr. the first time out. He is absolute dynamite."

Harry Foster: "...A whiz for shaping magnificent examples of how we live."

Paul Johnson: "This is a star who is so truly genuine he never exaggerates."

Arthur Campbell: "On your mark for a new brilliance."

Carl Rimes: "He is one of the most talented and exploratory entertainers around."

Stella Raymond: "Oscar Brown Jr. is one of the most dynamic artists in music today."

And yet, so much more acclaim was still to come. How also not to remember, mused Adam the while studying the ancient record jacket, a certain time in Washington some thirteen years later, when a declared admiration would be offered up to Oscar, in person, by the renowned orchestra conductor Samuel Ralston. Ralston, at the time, was in charge of certain productions at the Downtown Center and had just heard Oscar audition his musical, *Plantation,* by taking on each and every role and singing all of the lyrics. When the last note was sounded, Ralston rose from his chair, stepped forward to Oscar at the microphone and proclaimed what was generally accepted, and was destined to be so oft but inconsequentially repeated: "Mister Brown, you are truly a great artist and a genius."

But then, just as on innumerable other occasions, nothing came of all that esteem. Oscar managed no more than a mere one week run in Washington for his musical, and it didn't get staged at the Downtown Center but was put on rather amateurishly at the Wilson High School. Nothing more could be arranged for. If fault were to be placed, at least that time, it would surely not rest with Oscar.

It was disheartening, all too disheartening. Oscar, a superb musical composer, poetic lyricist, as well as performer, had deserved better. Tough enough, considered Adam, that the arts were by their very nature a sad enough endeavor to be part of for always falling somewhat short of the intended. By their inherent aims and their constant groping for escape from the ordinary to perfect spiritual kinds of experience, the arts seemed to strain everlastingly for a kind of emancipation not possible to achieve. That fact could be read in the look of every performer Adam had ever seen.

Still, putting such esoteric deliberation aside, and also not considering those artists who rightly or wrongly wound up having their creative efforts ridiculed or ignored, it was generally true that those finally drawing significant acclaim did manage to profit quite substantially. It was incredible that Oscar, for all the hyperbole of the kudos directed at him, had never gotten what ordinarily went with such recognition. And yet enormous amounts of money passed all too often to any number of performing mediocrities. It was no wonder, thought Adam, that Oscar would sometimes vent suspicions of a conspiracy of sorts operating against him and even have Adam wondering if the poor fellow wasn't on the right track.

Except for walking his dogs, Adam spent much of that day listening to favored tracks of Oscar's old records. Over the years, he had kept them all in chronological order.

For one recording dating back to about the mid-sixties Oscar was pictured in a joyful cover pose. That particular album stemmed from a joint effort with a Cuban composer, Ernesto Ricco. Ernesto, in fact, did mean a great deal to Oscar, both as a friend and as a person who introduced him to South American musical wellsprings destined to find their way into his own compositions and performances.

The cover had them together, with Oscar smiling and looking toward a presumably promising future. A few years later, Ernesto would die in a plane crash and Oscar would be pushing on. It was so characteristic of him. The man was undeterred by the paradox of being "great" yet not becoming a commercial success and doggedly, just kept "pushin' on."

Ernesto was not the only friend Oscar had found back then. Adam was another one.

What was happening to Adam now always occurred when Oscar was in town. Once they got together most of Adam's other preoccupations were set aside. It was much the same on this day. Adam's thoughts came to be less and less tainted by big bang pondering and were focused instead on Oscar's predicament.

If, after last night's gloomy telecast, he was inclined to hold nothing really worth bothering about, there remained, nevertheless, some part of him still singularly answerable and responsive to the demands of this long-standing relationship. A line from Oscar's featured song of the album with Ernesto Ricco seemed, on rehearing, to put an especially designing question to him. "Where's the helping hand for me?"

Christ. Responding to the implications and the challenge of that query stood to be a life-ending job at Adam's age and late stage of the game. Better to just knock out a quick book on Oscar Brown Jr. A book pointing up the injustice of his unfortunate slighting by the moguls of show business, and see what might come of floating it.

That was, if he could really manage to come up with such a book and somehow get it published.

Five

"You in a funky mood?"

Clare had appeared in the doorway and was taking a lead from yet another Oscar Brown Jr. recording. "In a Funky Mood" was still available, but only as a Japanese CD.

Over the years Clare had become just as familiar with Oscar's lyrics as Adam, the two of them having listened to his music often enough together. She had no taste for cabarets, however, and so pretty much left Adam to attend live performances by himself.

With a good voice of her own, it was not unusual for her to sound off at almost any time, in musical echo of Oscar's lines should Adam be listening to a record or whenever she might fancy it that a situation called for one of his pithy musical commentaries.

"No. I'm in the same old mood. But I've taken a pledge to boost his career."

"Well good. That's better than just hanging around here and moping. Is it to take pictures of his performances?"

Adam was an avid photographer. He'd made a point

of extensively photographing Oscar while on stage over the years.

"No. Not really."

"What then? A tape? You're going to record him again?"

"Nope. I've signed on to write a book about him. How does that grab you? A new wrinkle for me, hey?"

"You're kidding."

"Lady, this is no joke. And since when am I a kidder? It'll be his life story, but with an angle. Like, where's everybody been for all these years while he's been virtually starving save for empty praise? Like they say, there's an easy way to show appreciation. It was invented a long time ago and it's called money. So how about someone coming up with a little before it's too late?"

"But what do you know about writing a full length book? You can barely put together a short medical article because everything's got to be so god awful concise and to the minimalist point. Unless I'm mistaken, aren't you the guy who insists that anything really worth saying can be covered in a couple of pages, maybe even a couple of lines?"

"So it'll be a short book. With lots of quotes and also pictures. Any other comments?"

"Well, maybe it is a good idea. I'd sure like you to be doing something, anything, that'd make you happy. I pray for it every day."

"Yes. But it doesn't look like anyone is listening."

"You can't know that."

"Anyway. Happiness is a fantasy. It's not a reasonable expectation for us any more than for some other animal. But forget about me and think about Oscar. He's not looking for happiness. All he wants is to have enough money to do his own thing music wise and once in a while 'chill out'."

"You'd like a girl, Adam? Is that it? Would it help?"

"Excuse me? Maybe I missed some important part of this conversation. What the devil are you talking about?"

"C'mon. You know what I mean. It doesn't have anything to do with what we've been talking about. It's got to do with what I think may really be troubling you. So answer me. Is that what you need? For God's sake, don't hold back on my account."

"Look. I've got troubles enough without that kind also."

"It doesn't have to be troublesome."

"Yeah? What about AIDS, STDs and maybe having to talk to some young thing about love, and where some damned fool relationship might really be going? From what I've heard it could be the making of a disaster. Besides which, for guys my age, relationships have run out of steam. They can't go anywhere. That's if they make any sense, they're not. They're stayin' put. And that's where this one is stayin'. Right here, with you babe. You're quite enough for me. Always have been. Except for maybe a dream or two."

"There, see? I knew it."

"You don't know a damned thing. They were just non-descript wet dreams, and happened when you were out of town visiting your folks."

"I'll bet."

"Christ. First you give me the green light to fool around and now you're gonna fuss about a silly wet dream? Clare, you can't have it both ways. It's okay to hustle some dumb broad but not to have an innocent enough wet dream? That's crazy. How can you resent something that's just plain physiological?"

"I am not resenting anything and she doesn't have to

be a dumb broad. She could be a very nice girl. And that kind of a dream means you really are frustrated. What I'm only saying is that you don't have to be. Just because I don't care too much for that sort of thing anymore doesn't mean you have to be deprived."

"Look, lady. Or should I call you Madam Doctor Freud? The only things that have me frustrated right now are Oscar Brown Jr. and this absolutely stupid conversation we are having. So go and do something useful while I try to sort out my real problems. And in case you haven't noticed, I've become old and lack both the means and the time for nonsense. That includes sexual outings."

"I don't know about `means', Adam. So when would you like your lunch?"

"How about one o'clock? Or is that when you'll be feeding the dogs?"

"Oh I'll manage to squeeze you in somehow. You creep. But only because I love you. God, how I love you."

He had no doubt about that and wished she would leave off on this business of urging him to make out elsewhere. It had seemed to start off with innuendoes the year before, after Clare had developed ovarian cancer and undergone surgery followed by a prolonged course of chemotherapy. Ever since then, either directly or by inference, she'd have him enduring these embarrassingly persistent assurances of her release upon him.

For his part, although he'd occasionally fantasized such involvements, he'd found her prodding and proffered tolerance for such straying, quite bothersome. Especially since if he had even joked about such liaisons in earlier years, especially back when he was more sexually driven, she'd have had his head for it.

Her current sort of all too considerate needling was not at all welcome. It was oppressive enough for Adam to cope with the potentially serious consequences of his wife's illness without having also to contend with these far fetched self-sacrificial offerings, whatever their seeming practicality.

With Clare gone to the kitchen, Adam started up another of Oscar's records, chancing next to play a selection recorded in a sixties live performance at Blue's Alley in Washington. It was a lively song conveying a humorous but barbed rebuff of ill-concealed, mean-spirited white moves on blacks.

From the outset of his show business career, Oscar had opted for the role of maverick on racial issues. So no one knowing him would have been surprised to hear him insist, as he did in this particular number, that all he wanted for blacks was the accounting they'd been promised more than a century ago. That given, he was willing, and quite agreeably, to "hang mellow" and call the whole matter "square."

Adam had attended that particular performance at Blue's Alley and remembered how the crowd had roared to his lines. But it was mostly black people who were responding. The whites didn't seem to get it at all. They'd only come to hear Oscar's raucous and upbeat numbers. They were put off by this other business and didn't understand that when you got Oscar, you got the complete Oscar. And that he had to sing not only of his own experience but also of the entire black one. He was not about to omit or except any part of it even if, all too unfortunately, that's what it took to be a commercial success in the days before belligerent forms of hip-hop came along and changed the scene quite substantially.

Adam was quite aware that this inclination on Oscar's part constituted a substantial career stumbling block. Especially since more than one observant pundit had opined that Oscar was forever violating what at that time constituted an unwritten show biz understanding, to whit, performing artists do not get political, particularly in racial ways, when on stage. But that was exactly the unique posture Oscar had struck for himself from the very beginning.

Back then no one else had dared it. Other performers appreciated that they could get away with almost anything if they kept it a nonprofessional matter, on their own time, and apart from their performances. They could even promote profitable hair-brained ventures or all sorts of notorious advocacy. Dick Gregory had diet salad dressings and went on protest fasts. Jane Fonda went to Hanoi to sympathize with the North Vietnamese. Miriam Makeba embraced the thinking of Stokely Carmichael and wound up marrying the man.

On stage, though, these artists just saw to their first order of business, that of providing entertainment. After all, the conventional acceptance was that when people were out for a good time they didn't want to hear about someone else's problems. What more natural than that the money managers of the booking agencies and recording industry should demand consistent good vibrations, and not good vibrations interspersed with even an occasional racial crack or inference? God forbid then that there should be an outright racially slanted aspersion or slur.

That was what Adam was led to understand whenever

he ran into people in show business management. People like Sam Berk, a New York agent who had chaperoned dozens of famous performers through lucrative careers and who had gotten negative comments about Oscar from long time contacts at the influential William Morris Agency in New York. When those fellows signed up an artist, they didn't want to be worrying about risk-benefit ratios. They wanted as close to a sure thing as could be arranged for and no unforeseeable risks, period.

So when old, truth-baring Oscar broke out with numbers describing your average day as a black man in jail, or what it was like to wake up in a ghetto, it did not matter if the rest of that recording or that night's performance was so much slap-happy fun or touching lyricism. Oscar would find himself in deep trouble.

Still, why might it be taken for granted by those holding the purse strings that a white audience would go for Gershwin's *Porgy and Bess* but not for Oscar's *Plantation*, a better play on a similar theme and probably just as good musically? Something else had to be going on. And the presumable difference lay in the racial politics of a composer who, first and foremost, was an upstart black man.

What Oscar Brown Jr. did was to remind whites, back then, all too vividly what it was like to be black in white America. When he sang he never let go on that experience choosing to epitomize it to the nth degree even should his act find him joking about some other thing. His overriding purpose was to project the essence of what such an existence amounted to and how it felt.

Oscar never confused that issue or blurred that image, which is what most other black performers had wound up doing. They might do a black thing, too, but they did it on white society's terms and usually in its manner. That was the only way a Sammy Davis, Jr., or a Harry Belafonte or a Sidney Poitier could get ahead in 60's white America. Those performers had pretty much learned the punishing lesson taught to Paul Robeson years before.

Adam recognized that there were a few black, often no talent performers, who had made out for awhile with mindless racist outbursts of inflammatory, threatening, even vitriolic content. There was a limited market for that kind of quick transient notoriety or vulgar spectacle. But they faded fast and had really nothing to say. Such entertainers, including the most blatantly angry ones didn't even manage to bother too many white people because they hardly stood to be around for very long and represented little of anything but primitive raw feelings.

What made musical industry executives truly uneasy and what for them was most alarming was a perfectly phrased and rhythmic melody, somewhat abstract and slyly softened, but all the same a disturbing representation of fundamental racial truths. That kind of blackness was not suitable for a prospective commercial sell, irrespective of how convincingly inspired or gifted the creative artist. The worse for Oscar Brown Jr., truth by real art expressed is more threatening than raw vituperation, the latter usually being either ignored or taken for ludicrous. And Oscar, to echo Samuel Ralston's ringing declaration, was not only a great artist but in fact "a genius" who could readily mount that kind of creative wizardry.

So Oscar, according to Adam (a reasonable book title?), was from the very beginning to the present the quintessential entertainer of inescapably assertive blackness in a white man's world.

Ruefully, Adam reminded himself of Oscar's light-hearted but poignant lyric on the consequence of that state of affairs: "Can I get a dime? Can I get a dime? I'm a dime away from a hot dog, two bucks away from a bed. All sorts of funky pictures runnin' around in my head" and on and on and on. When and how would it all play out?

Would it do so abruptly, devastatingly, or as finally it now seemed, merely wind down as just one other futile life effort? Adam could easily foresee his friend sitting somewhere on a run-down park bench, demeaned by an unappreciative music industry and yet single-mindedly ignoring it all to scribble away on his writing pad so as to polish off a five hundredth song that no one would ever get to hear. Or perhaps, once again, he'd be as he'd seen him years ago on a Philadelphia street corner, downcast, tearful for all of his futile pounding against unyielding show business doors, and requiring a handout.

It was time for lunch, whether or not Adam could muster the appetite for it.

Six

Samantha, Adam's Doberman, was crowding the kitchen table. Chicken, however served, was her passion. Adam had to force his way past her for those cold leftovers which were to be his own claim. Kelly, the wolfhound, although towering over the Dobe, hung back his usual respectful distance, and waited on what leavings might escape her voracious, never satisfied longings. Clare was boiling water for Adam's tea.

"How's it going, Mister Big Deal Biographer?"

"It'll never work."

"Writer's block already?"

"Very funny. I'm nowhere near to putting anything down on paper. I've only been sitting around, spinning records, thinking about Oscar's career, and casting about for what might be a good approach, some kind of selling angle for such a book that would help me get started. But I'm up against the same old difficulty.

"When you come right down to it, there's always that same tough hurdle with Oscar, the charge that he's not commercial and that's because invariably he rubs the guys who run everything in his business the wrong way. And you want to know something? That's crazy as hell because he's never had any real difficulty with anyone else. Not even white audiences. They're usually quite satisfied to sit through some of his racial pitches in order to enjoy the other parts of his act. I don't believe it's an exaggeration to say that most white audiences usually wind up being enthralled. It's only the agency people and the producers who've taken it upon themselves to see if they can't tone him down some, and always failing in that, they throw up their hands and wind up blackballing him.

"What I'm starting to wonder is, if he couldn't sell those guys on his routine thirty years ago, how the devil would some book written about him now, however flattering or even favorably reviewed, stand to reverse their kind of thinking? He sure as hell hasn't changed any. He's still singing about black culture and black history in the same old way, and like always, they're gonna say he's too `messagey.' Oscar and the purse string guys have worked themselves into opposing corners.

"The pity of it all is that if only they would give him half a chance and showcase him once in awhile, his career would probably take off and everybody would clean up."

"So you won't do it?"

"Not so fast. I'm only venting."

"Sounds more like you're looking for an excuse to not even get started."

"Clare. Are you out to needle me? Go on, keep it up. I'm planning to let him down. Right?"

"I'll shut up. I'm sure you know what's best."

"Now you're really getting to me."

Clare was a master at it. The idea was to say something

one way, the while intending and rather expecting it to be taken another. Then she would find ways to reinforce what had only been implicit, she in such case being the actual one to know what was best or inevitable.

"Now Adam, you know very well that once you say you're going to do something, sooner or later you are going to do it, no matter what. You can't just not do it. So stop beating about the bush. Settle down and get to work. And if you wind up doing nothing more than pleasing Oscar, it will have been well worth doing it, anyway."

To please Oscar? That was a far cry from how Adam had viewed this writing project when he'd ventured the idea of it. And now all he could really think about was not upsetting the poor man should he fail to make good on his commitment.

But might that be what a tedious year of conceiving, typing, and proof reading would actually come down to? Just Oscar's satisfaction with his having made the effort, however futile the whole thing turned out? And would Oscar really be satisfied, if with the book before the public, his career still failed to come alive and begin to pay off?

Adam knew it was assured. Oscar would get a perverse kick out of it. He always reveled in ironical humor and could find a light side to anything. It was one of his saving strengths. But for Adam, a failure to accomplish little more than to hand Oscar something else to joke about didn't take too well.

"That's what I'm supposed to do? I'm supposed to work my ass off just to please Oscar?"

"What's so bad about that?"

It was an interesting question. And one he'd certainly have to mull over. Things needing to be mulled over were sort of piling up. But at this point, he'd become tired of fighting the dogs for scraps and fencing with Clare.

"I'm going back inside. Thanks for the scraps and the advice."

"Don't mention it."

Once returned to the den, he opened Oscar's envelope. His friend had enclosed a chronology of recordings and performances. There was also a resumé headed "OSCAR BROWN JR." It made interesting reading.

But at no more than first glance, the incongruities of this curriculum vitae could get any discerning reader down. Here was Oscar, a gifted person looking as great on paper as in the flesh. And maybe he'd also be great in some kind of final accounting. But right now, if the sum of his achievements were to be totaled up in the dollars and cents of the entertainment world, he wasn't making out any better, possibly even worse, than those just starting out.

Money wise, he was at the lowest rung of the compensation ladder. And, sad to say, Oscar had been on stage for over forty years. For all of his having managed to become "a legend in his own time," there was no more practical comfort in that than if it might also be finally and later agreed to, that he was one of those performing greats to wind up being cheated because they were born before a more propitious moment.

Now here was still another thing to chew on. The transparently implausible business of some kind of ultimate summing up. How, conceivably, could he still be thinking along such lines? It apparently remained all too easy to fall back on his old ways of thinking. But why should that be? Did he not at last know, and therefore accept, there would be no final kinds of accounting? Finality no longer promised the possibility of anything. Oscar, Clare, and he, along with all of their remains and feeble scratchings, were going to simply vaporize and disappear.

Christ, then why bother with any of this? To do no more than briefly please Oscar? Had Clare come up with an awful but simple truth? Life was about a few moments, and not persistence?

A glum Adam had to get out of the house. He called to the wolfhound and led him away. Together, they spent the afternoon hiking over horse trails in Rock Creek Park.

Dogs were such fantastically efficient creatures. Never so foolish as to get overextended or to be involved with the implausible, they were in perfect synch with nature. When it was time, dogs drank exactly the amount of water required. Forever nosing the ground, they determined precisely, infallibly, what it was they had to know just by the way things smelled.

And never did they appear to live on the need for anything like self-esteem or general kinds of acceptance. A single admiring master could fill their bill perfectly. Narrowly focused, they settled for looking to their immediate needs, expectancies, provocations, aversions. Dogs might see the moon, but never would they reach for it.

Adam could guess at Oscar's reaction to his animals' sense of completion.

"Well, I ain't no damned dog."

Seven

The Barry Theater was usually booked for performances of rock music, but tonight it was leased out for the Ninth Annual Black Entertainers Benefit Series. Adam had seen Oscar make charitable appearances over the years, but from his point of view, such limited exposure to usually small audiences did little to stimulate any appreciation of his talent. And unfortunately, his sets under such circumstances often suffered from a lack of both proper design and competent backup musicians.

Adam could recall one unfortunate event in the lounge of a student dormitory amid clouds of cigarette smoke and the buzz of inattentive collegiate chatter where musical accompaniment had not even been provided.

On this particular evening, however, the theater was a recently erected modern structure and there was a competent trio to provide musical support.

Adam arrived, as had been suggested, thirty minutes before the second show. After buying his ticket, he browsed his way past photographs of noted rock stars smiling or leering down from the lobby walls and several vending

booths with featured offerings of all sorts of African trin-
kets and artifacts.

A crowd of theatergoers, also waiting for the second
show, was building in the lobby. It was entirely made up
of African Americans, there not being a single Caucasian
face among them. Although blacks did constitute the core
of Oscar's following, tonight, among those who were gathered, there were not many of his actual fans. The big draw
here was the charitable endeavor and the opportunity for
social hobnobbing, not an appreciation of Oscar's artistry.

Adam moved forward to look at a television monitor
mounted on the wall so that people in the lobby could
check what was going on inside the theater. He could
barely hear what was happening on stage, but sure enough,
there was Oscar looking quite animated about something.

Rather than continue to stand around outside, and
having determined that the theater was about half-empty,
he prevailed upon an usher to yield him early entry and
as Oscar's specially "invited friend," let him catch the tail
end of the first show.

Heading forward along the center aisle, in short order,
Adam was transported. That was how Oscar, one or another
way, always managed to affect him. Adam felt himself carried back a long twenty-six years and to what he'd heard
back then at the Ellington Theater in Chicago.

It was that same song now and the same voice, if out
of an older-appearing Oscar. It happened to be true, just as
Oscar had insisted a few hours earlier, that his voice was
in fact "better and stronger than ever." He was doing his
"Brother Where Are You?" number, another favorite from
his extensive repertoire.

Usually a crowd pleaser and generally apropos, it was

not the case, at least for Adam this time, because of the peculiar manner in which Oscar was delivering the song as he closed out his first set.

"A small boy walked down a city street and hope was in his eyes, as he searched the faces of the people he'd meet for one he could recognize. Brother where are you? They told me that you came this way. Brother where are you? They said you came this way... They said you came this way. Brother, brother, brother, where are you... ?"

Because Adam's microphone-clutching friend up there, stooping forward in order to overhang the edge of the stage apron, was staring straight down at him, but with feigned, pop-eyed, astonishment as Adam made his way along the aisle. What was Oscar's purpose in doing this? Was it to suggest to everyone seated nearby that Adam was the unavailingly awaited, never to arrive "brother"?

Then Oscar began to search out faces in the audience and to nod at them collusively as affirming that yes this was the one, the one at which to indeed point the finger of blame for all kinds of black adversity, this one presently coming down the aisle. Adam was the culprit and the problem, Oscar's problem, their problem.

How absurdly unfair. Why was Oscar doing this? Why had he chosen to embarrass him? Adam did not take kindly to any insinuation he'd not heard that small boy's cry. For it was precisely his having heard it well enough that had occasioned his very being there. That's why he'd always been there through all of his and Oscar's years together and apart. Was it not a fact that whenever something had been asked of him, he could be counted on? Or was it that this musically expressed aspersion concerned Adam's hesitancy to write the book?

Oh well, maybe he was reading too much into typical Oscar Brown Jr. high jinks or was it just this song? It always had its way of getting to you, of cutting right through to the issue of wherefore no actual brotherhood, and of doing it unsparingly.

With the audience now emptying out, Adam moved forward to renew his acquaintance, and to exchange pleasantries with some of Oscar's relatives whom he'd spotted sitting close by. Then he went backstage.

Oscar was taking his break in the company of the master of ceremonies for the evening, a certain Willy Hancock. Hancock, who headed up the music department at Morgan State University, had known Oscar since the late fifties, and was a performer of jazz in his own right.

What Adam could hear of their conversation seemed all very superficial and upbeat. You would never suspect from listening that the struggle for Oscar's last chance to make good was at that very same time in progress. Adam, having no taste for this somewhat phony conviviality, made his way back into the theater and was feeling himself the melancholy witness to a preposterous charade.

He returned to a front row seat and along with a new audience was soon having to endure the second set preliminaries. There were typical fundraising pitches from speakers seeming to glory in their sudden privilege of a brief turn in the limelight and holding a restless audience captive. As usual, they ran unduly long.

After that, several good songs were belted out by a young, aspiring female vocalist. Next to come on was a towering black actor-singer locally known for his leaning toward Paul Robeson musical favorites. But on this occasion he chose, instead, to deliver a somewhat obscure, yet nonetheless distinctly unpleasant racist diatribe. With an impressively sonorous speaking voice and commanding presence, he might very well have done justice to Shakespeare instead of his spew of raw invective. Adam thought, that he celebrated himself a little too much to boot, and was glad when he finished and exited from the stage.

Finally, at last, came Oscar's introduction. Freddy Hancock was kindly indulgent. He called Oscar a master and pronounced him to be the essence of what it meant to be "cool," to be, as a matter of fact, "Mr. Cool himself."

Adam couldn't help thinking that here was probably a man in good position to do a lot more for Oscar than to merely turn up, like tonight, in order to render faint praise at a small-time benefit performance. But fellows like him had their own agenda and to Adam's eye, entertainers were especially apt to be jealous of another's career success by virtue of their narcissistic ways. To be in show business, in fact, was not to be in a particularly friendly place at all. He could remember how consistently mean spirited he'd observed a certain comedian to be as soon as he vacated the stage.

Almost forty-five minutes were consumed before Oscar came on again. Except for an introductory piece involving lyrics he'd written for music by Teddy Wilson, he stayed with old and once popular favorites. Adam marveled at how Oscar had retained, in spite of his age, so much of the agility required for numbers which imposed quite athletic demands upon him.

It was an enthusiastic yet restrained audience. Adam thought it in keeping with the way people generally reacted when they had one kind of anticipation, or mind set, and then were exposed to the unexpected, no matter how wondrously well it had turned out. How could it be otherwise tonight? After all, these people were there to rub elbows with one another, to sport their new outfits, and to congratulate themselves for being charitable in support of a worthy cause. They weren't there to admire and to acclaim the wonder of Oscar Brown Jr.

Adam had also gone off recently to watch Oscar perform in a small Virginia club. That audience, made up largely of weekenders getting together for drinks and gossip, had been so noisy and inattentive that Oscar couldn't even bring himself to go back on for a scheduled second set.

Well, what was really to be expected nowadays? The poor man had only one recording still out there for sale. So how was he to recruit new fans? And those of his own era were by now either homebound grandparents or dead.

Unfortunately, as tonight, he'd been reduced to a limited and lackadaisical kind of public exposure. One could sense a kind of funereal air to it.

Following what Adam considered to be an especially dynamic performance, ending again to the strains of "Brother Where Are You," Oscar drew only a single curtain call and there were none of the old and customary kinds of applause or shouts for an encore.

Adam had had quite enough of this awkward audience reserve and rose disgustedly to head for home, not intending to spend any further time with Oscar or his family that evening. He needed quiet distance now, wanting to give this night's experience time to sink in and to await what might come of it, as a means for tooling up his stab at authorship, or somehow eliciting those mysteriously sad but pleasurable feelings he'd had the previous night. But he didn't really think there was a reasonable prospect for such contrivances. The right kind of stimulation had simply failed to develop. The atmosphere attending the evening's performance by his friend was a non-conducive downer.

"Sir?"

Someone smelling nice had tapped him on the right shoulder from behind. He twisted around to investigate and just about instantly found himself wondering if his pessimistic attitude had been premature.

The approach was from a young woman whom he knew blacks were apt, at one time, to call honey-skinned. More importantly, she was provocatively configured and good looking enough for him to grasp at once, that just like that, there could be a problem.

"I was watching you," she sort of whispered. "Are you an old friend of the Brown family?"

"Things do get worse and worse. Don't they? Thirty years ago someone like yourself took me for an impressario. But you're right. I'm just an old, old friend. And who would you happen to be?"

"Charlene Davis. I'm a freelance writer and I was thinking of doing something on Mr. Brown."

"Well first off, don't call him Mr. Brown. It's got a wrong ring to it. Call him Oscar, or Oscar Brown Jr. Anyway, what do you have in mind? Do you want to actually do him some good or are you just out to write another one of those dumb articles reading like an obituary?"

Charlene Davis let his queries pass. She smiled in a knowing manner, maybe a little invitingly to his thinking, and pressed on.

"Hey, mister. I like your style. You are a real friend, aren't you?"

Adam had begun to consider that maybe he was on to something other than the woman's configuration. He decided to become less confrontational.

"Is there something you want to know?"

"Well, how would all of this come off in the old days, like twenty years ago? I did manage to catch him on network TV last year and one other time on Public Broadcasting..."

"That was acting, or doing interviews. Hardly the real Oscar. For things like that he was just doing what it took to make a buck."

"Well I finally did succeed in getting a hold of one of his LPs. It was a blast. But you know what? I had to buy it used. It wasn't in stock, anywhere."

"So you understand the problem, right?"

"Sure. But why? He's fantastic."

"It's not a short story. Where are you heading now?"

"I'm gonna cab home."

"Where's that?"

"Columbia and 16th."

"Well if you like, I can drop you off and we can talk on the way. I don't live far from you."

"Okay. You sure it's no trouble?"

"Not in the least."

What at first had been but a kernel, seemed suddenly ready to burst forth. The idea continued to grow as he spoke.

"In fact, you might be the one to wind up sparing me a lot of trouble."

"I don't follow you."

Maybe she would. Follow his lead. It could happen. This gal might just be his deliverance, the way out of a tough situation. Here, unexpectedly and without current precedent, was someone probably just dying to write Oscar up.

Could he start feeding her all of the old material, the albums, his live tapings of shows no one even remembered, and see if she, under his direction, would do not a mere article, but a whole damned book? He might have himself exactly the right pigeon. Which would leave him free of his obligation to Oscar and full time for Clare, his dogs, and those implications of the big bang problem needing to be sorted out.

Stealing a few observant glances at her as he led the way across K Street to his parked car, he couldn't help but feel rather pleased that his potential pigeon was a damned good looking one at that. In short order they were on their way. Going to the Barry Theater tonight was turning out to be not such a bad idea, after all.

"What have you published?"

Whatever his initial enthusiasm, no point in spinning his wheels with someone who for lack of experience couldn't make good on such an arrangement, then only having to work even harder trying his own hand at it later on. That would be worse than just settling down right now and facing up to the task himself.

"Well, I did an article last week on Miles Davis for the *Village Voice*. There was a short piece on Mingus in the *Post* and I'm planning something on Dizzy for the *New Yorker*. It's his seventy-fifth this year. Did you know that?"

"You putting me on?"

"About what?"

"All these published things. You look so young. By the way, my name is Adam. Adam Grossman."

"Hello, Adam Grossman."

He suspected she was now eyeing him more closely, kind of sizing him up. He reserved his own gaze for the road, especially since it had started to rain and his windshield wipers, which should have been changed months ago, were objecting and streaking badly.

"How old are you, anyway?"

"Hey, I haven't even gotten to mention my book on Louis Armstrong."

The car lurched to the right until Adam regained control.

"You've published a book on Louis Armstrong?"

"No. I really had you going there, didn't I? You almost had us up on the sidewalk."

The handsome girl of barely black color had a genuinely happy kind of laugh.

"Sorry. I didn't mean to pry but to be quite frank, you're handing me all this stuff about what you've written on musical personalities and I'm thinking of making you a proposition. That's if you're interested and I'm convinced you're up to it."

"Hey, man."

She laughed again good-heartedly, and so attractively, that he began to wonder the full extent of what he was actually getting himself into.

"Look. Right now, Oscar doesn't need some kind of a short article. He needs a whole book. And if I could recruit someone to do it and it had a reasonable chance of success, I'm in a position to deliver whatever background material would be needed. Whoever did the writing wouldn't have to do any research at all. All they'd have to do is sit down and do the writing."

"Like I say, my name is Charlene Davis." She reached

across, patting his right hand softly where it rested on the wheel. "And if you want, you and I have a deal, Mr. Adam Grossman. Let's see, what else was it you needed to know? Right, I remember. Charlene is twenty-nine, going on thirty next month. So what do you say, am I or am I not your girl?"

Adam wasn't entirely sure of the full intent of that question.

"I'd have to see some of your material. And of course I'd need to run this kind of arrangement past Oscar."

"No problem. You're quite a stickler for details, aren't you, Adam? Okay, that's my building over there on the right. I'll just hop out on the corner. Here you go. It's my phone number. I'm writing it down on this piece of paper."

She placed it on the armrest between them.

"I'd better see you to the door. It's not too well lit out there."

"No need. I'll be just fine. Let me know if Oscar makes with the green light. Then you can see if I write the way you want. I can get started almost any time. Don't lose my number now."

Even though it was dark, Adam could see well enough to appreciate the way she walked. A fine example of a certain kind of grace.

If this Charlene could write as well as she spoke, looked, and walked, he might indeed have himself quite a deal. He was glad that Charlene had not invited him upstairs to her place right then and there, to talk it over some more, or to show him samples of what she'd written. He'd surely have gone, and it was much too late for that.

Eight

As usual, not one for much sleep, Oscar was on the phone to him early. Adam was still in bed.

"Where'd you disappear to last night?"

"We've got to talk. I met this woman."

"Think I didn't see that chick? How was it?"

"Nothing like that. She's a writer."

"Yeah? Well she sure wasn't takin' any notes last night. What she was doin', from how I saw it, was layin' fer you, Adam old boy."

"Mind if I proceed?"

"Go on, say your piece but remember I know all there is to know about foxy ladies."

"Look. She's a writer and done articles, published ones, on some really big time musicians, Miles, Dizzy, Mingus. Better still, she thinks you're hot stuff. And get this. She's got both the inclination and the time. So why don't we give her a shot at it?"

"You're talkin' about... ?"

"What else? Sure. The book."

"Shit no!"

"Why the hell not? It's like providential. She's deep and heavy into that sort of thing and I'd only be struggling. Besides, I can set it up so she only gets the material I feed her. And it wouldn't be like her having a free hand. The two of us would be working on it together and your story would not only be authentic, but have a professional ring to it."

"Adam. Am I gonna have to tell you what's really on your mind? And let's just drop all this far out stuff about her representin' some neat bit of providence. Look man. I've been there. Heard everythin' these sweet talkin' chicks put out. An' then some. First, all they want is to get your attention. Make you a little curious. Next thing you know, you're gettin' it on together. And then... Gotcha! Before you realize what's happened, it's, 'Could we do this? Could we do that?' Not to mention all the 'Gimmee, gimmee, gimmee.' And they can be so tricky, and so slippery, like teflon. Whoeee! Hey, brother. You notice this one didn't come on to me directly for this so-called write-up? You can bet she damn well knew better. Knew I'd a' sent her packin' to a fare thee well. You bein' set up, Adam, and haven't got a clue to what's goin' on."

"What's that supposed to mean?"

Adam didn't appreciate the idea he was some kind of patsy. Yet Oscar kept laying it on.

"She just took you fer' easier than me, you know, a soft touch. She was takin' no chances because I'da known just where she was comin' from. I can spot a scam a long ways off. But you, old buddy, you still don't get it, do you? A smart guy like you. It's criminal. So listen up. Fer' maybe writin' a coupla' lines, if that, she's gonna try and have herself a windfall."

"For Christ's sake, Oscar, aren't you losing track of a whole bunch of things? First off, nobody's ballin' anyone."

"Maybe not yet they ain't... You're just beginnin' to get sucked in. That's all. This kinda' chick spins webs."

"Look. Let's say you've got it nailed down correctly. Let's say your paranoia is right on the money. And one way or another, she gets to connive her way into either doing nothing at all or just comes up with some kind of a short piece about you. She never makes good on a book. What in hell would be so terrible about that? You've had writers who've copped out on you entirely, or given you no more than passing mention."

"Bingo. Right. Now you're talkin'. Because none of that has ever done me any fuckin' good or we wouldn't be in the shape we are presently in. And when those cats did write me up, they wound up gettin' a nice piece of change for the little they put out. But not me. Not yours truly. I didn't see any fuckin' difference in either my pocket or the number of bookin's comin' my way.

"No, Adam. We've got a better way now, thanks to you. You went and got yourself a real cool idea. That we do it in house, so to speak, on our very own. And we control it from the get-go. Maybe then we'll get some-where, especially if the story's true to life, and even half-well put together, and it gets served up as a full-sized book. 'Course now, mind you, we've got no gripe if you want to just go ahead and lay the bitch. But otherwise we are just goin' to stick to our original plan and play it all close to the vest.

"Which brings up another thing. We don't take too kindly to the idea of you handin' over all our private tapings to anyone who just happens to come along. That's privileged material, man. No tellin' what could happen if it falls into the wrong hands."

"That's an awful lot of we-in', Oscar. Whatcha mean we? Hell, it's only me. I'm the one who's actually got to sit down and write the thing, maybe even have to put in a year or more at it. What with trying to get it written and then seeing that it's peddled right, it could even take longer. And suppose you're dead wrong. Suppose she's the real article. Then, what would be so wrong about using the woman? I still say, she could be heavenly sent. And all our material stays protected if when we start out, although she does the writing, I maintain control of everything. Oscar, this woman could be a big plus. If not providence then call it a gift horse. How's that for you? You like that better? Look. At the very least, let's have a peek at what she's written and find out who her contacts are? Who the hell do you or I know with publishing house connections?"

It was a phone conversation, but Adam could visualize Oscar shaking his head ruefully.

"You've got to get in her pants, don't you?"

"Hell. I haven't done anything like that for an eternity. And I don't believe she's out to play me for a sucker."

"You don't think you forgot how, do you?"

"Come off it, Oscar. Let's get practical."

"What's her name?"

He had calmed down. Or maybe he was about to slip off into one of his rejuvenating naps.

"Charlene Davis."

"Never heard of her."

"So we'll all get famous together. It could happen."

"You won't give her any of the original recordings or

your tapes of my shows. It all stays with us. Have I got it right?"

"Hell. I can't believe I'm hearing this. Since when did you ever hold on to anything? I'm the one who keeps the archives, remember? I promise you this. You've got my word on it. She gets nothing but cassette copies. I'll feed them to her one at a time and see to it, personally, that everything comes back."

"Okay, but I'm still thinkin' you don't know what's goin' on in your own head. I'll talk to you by the end of the week. And guess what? I lined up a two-night gig and maybe a commercial jingle in L.A.. I'll be takin' the red eye tonight."

Practicing surgery was easy compared to being retired like this. As a surgeon, Adam had been used to straight-forwardly determining exactly what needed to be done. Then he would proceed with it. Now, it looked like he was beginning to do nothing but scheme over how to do as little as possible about this damned book.

Also, he was flabbergasted when he began to appreciate that he was dealing with three people, not one of whom had an exact idea of what he was actually up to. Oscar didn't know he was urgently searching for ways out of writing the book, mostly because he needed time to dwell on how he fitted in with an unexpectedly revealed abysmal order of things. Charlene might not fully appreciate, whatever her wiles, that he would not have been quite so enthusiastic were she not as good looking as she was. And Clare couldn't possibly imagine how much he wondered if she was truly serious about wanting him to look for sexual diversion. And how would she respond if he took her up on it? Let alone how much grilling and needling he would have to endure should he so much as mention the existence of a Charlene.

Suddenly he'd become the central dissembling character in a convoluted plot of uncertain ending and his life had become altogether too complicated and worse, unpredictable. Every last bit of this because he had acted impulsively out of a quick and ready disposition to lend aid to a friend. So much to have been set in motion in less than twenty-four hours. Incredible.

Once more it would be Clare trying any which way to get him out of bed.

"It's a lovely day, Adam. Why don't you go sailing?"

"Because I'm in bed, and besides, I hate sailing."

"So sell it. Get rid of that stupid boat."

"I can't. I've come to hate sailing but I still love boats and after all it does belong to me. Or maybe I belong to it. Don't you get it? There's no one else who would ever care for it like I do. Besides, how can you sell off your own fiberglass and blood? You have no heart."

"Okay, don't go sailing. Just get out of bed and we'll take it from there."

"Why do I have to get out of bed? I know that Oscar's not downstairs. He was just on the phone to me."

"That's nice. You two getting together later about the book?"

"Not today. Anyway, he's heading for California. He's found a gig and one of those TV commercials they pay him peanuts for."

"He should insist on more money."

"Yeah? Then he wouldn't get the work at all."

"Do you know what they actually wind up paying him for those things?"

"I asked once and he was too embarrassed to say."

"Adam, you've simply got to do something for that poor man."

Adam was thinking, God forbid she should find out precisely how he was setting about it.

"I'm getting up, if only to escape you."

"And to start writing?"

"Nag, nag, nag. How much is Oscar paying you to keep after me?"

"He has no money for that. It's money he needs. Remember?"

"I know. I know. I simply must settle down and do the right thing. Correct? To please Oscar. To please you. Have you once considered I might prefer to do something else today?"

"You said you wouldn't go sailing."

"I've changed my mind. I'm going after all. Maybe it will clear my head."

It wasn't that sailing stood to clear his head. He'd hit on an innovative idea. And it would save him from having to get together with Charlene in her apartment. Right now, looking at Clare, that was something he could not bring himself to do. Instead, he'd go sailing and have Charlene along.

When Clare had gone downstairs, he made the call.

Nine

Charlene came on the run, taking her seat alongside him with unmistakable eagerness. She'd followed his lead on what to wear, but for her sneakers and jeans to be so dazzlingly white was more than he'd bargained for. It smacked of carefree excess and this was supposed to be a businesslike, down-to-earth intercession of one older man in the cause of another. Besides which, his boat, used so infrequently and somewhat neglected, was sure to need a liberal hosing down.

These downbeat ruminations were dissipated by his sighting of a small manilla folder tucked in the crook of her right arm which appeared to be stuffed with a considerable number of printed pages.

"Wow. I've never been on a sailboat before. Where's it at?"

"Annapolis. We can make it in an hour."

"All that way? Gee. I figured we were just heading for the Potomac."

"I'm afraid not. I gave up sailing on the river years ago. There's not enough steady wind, the water's too shallow, and about all you can do is tack back and forth over very short distances."

"What's that?"

"Tacking?"

"Yes."

"Sorry. It's like zig-zagging. You're stuck with it on the river because the wind almost never blows straight across. It's always coming from the north or south and the river is quite narrow. So all you can do is tack back and forth for what seems forever and not make much headway. But out on the bay you don't have that kind of a problem. Whichever way the wind happens to be blowing there's always plenty of room to set a course and then you can generally stick with it for quite awhile. If you want, I can explain some of the other basics once we're on board. That's unless you don't have time to drive all the way out there."

"Can I get home by seven?"

"Sure. Easily. Even if we're back by six, we'll still have a good four hours of sailing. And by the time you've heard me out on Oscar, you'll probably think it's more like eight. Just don't let me forget, once we're back, to give you the cassette tapes. They're locked in the trunk."

"Like I said last night. You're so precise and fussy about everything, aren't you? Anyway, I brought these samples of my writing you wanted to look at. So how'm I doin' so far, Adam? Do I at least get an A for effort?"

Adam had the idea that although she appeared to be making light of their situation, all the same, she'd been looking him over rather intently every chance she got.

"Exactitude is force of habit with me. Once upon a time I was a doctor."

"No kidding? What kind?"

"Chest surgery. Heart and blood vessels."

"That's neat. My sister is in pediatric nursing."

"That's not so neat. Kids are kinda messy."

They laughed, awkwardly, falsely. Enough so for her to quickly change the subject back to Oscar.

"So he's for it? My doing the book?"

"No, actually. It took a lot of persuasion and we haven't quite settled it. First, I'm to look at how you've written up those other people. And you ought to know it right now, because sooner or later you'll probably hear it from him, he'd rather I did the book, not you."

"So why don't you?"

"Because I don't know the first thing about that kind of writing. And right now I need time for other things."

Charlene fairly jumped for clarification of that little divulgence.

"Like what, Adam?"

Hardly an easy one to answer.

"I'm not quite sure. That's the problem. It needs sorting out. Let's just say it may be important."

"Your old lady giving you a hard time?"

"No. Not at all. Hey. You some kind of investigative reporter? I thought show business was your angle."

"Sorry. It's just the nosey woman in me coming out. I didn't mean to butt in, if it's too personal."

They were already eastbound on Route 50. It was a warm spring day and Adam had opened his sunroof widely enough to allow the occasional glimpse of brush-worked clouds as well as overhanging trees in early blossom.

He could sense that once again she'd taken to sizing him up and had also noticed that the air being drawn through the cracked sunroof was becoming distinctly perfumed within the car's interior. He found himself not minding it, nor that her curiosity had turned personal. He just hoped that further words between them would skirt any delving, particularly during these pleasantly scented moments, into where the universe might be headed. The recounting of such concerns could seem flat-out screwy.

"Everything is personal. Let's just say it's not anything mysterious, and let it go at that."

Like hell it wasn't.

"I wouldn't know about mysterious. I'm a very practical-minded, a hands-on kind of person."

He wished she hadn't put it that way. It brought to mind the last night's brief touch of her hand upon his. Easy enough to guess the softness of those hands.

"Perfect. That's exactly what this job description calls for. Someone who'll take a no-nonsense approach, get down to business, and grind out Oscar's story."

"Just like that? Wouldn't we need some kind of an angle to make it sort of special?"

"Sure. I'm glad you thought of that. It would go something like this. Let's, before it's all too late, get with it and celebrate what we've got in this fellow, Oscar Brown Jr. And before he's just another Scott Joplin. You know what I mean, born before his time. Oscar even sings about situations like that. And every time he does, it knocks me out. All I have to do is think of him on stage singing some sad prediction about his own future and it gets to me. Songs like that are terrible downers."

Adam looked drearily forward through the windshield, the while shaking his head.

"Hey man. Come out of it."

She was snapping her fingers before his nose.

"Lighten up. You can really get scary, you know that? I'm beginning to think you might even get an upbeat person like me down. I got your point. Take my word for it and ease off a little. One thing I've learned is that it never pays to get all hung up and carried away on a bad trip."

"Well, you wanted to know the angle. So now you have it. Our book, by way of publicizing Oscar's predicament, is to be an end-run rescue mission. If we don't manage to pull it off, then money wise, it's going to stay nothing but crying time for him from here on in. And unless you can build a sense of urgency into this, that this is a desperate last chance for him, and proceed in that frame of mind, then the whole damned business won't count for anything. Somehow we've got to make his career profitable in the here and now. Whatever they say about it, today's legend doesn't generally get to pay tomorrow's bills. So think it over. That's what you have to accomplish. Otherwise, forget it."

At the risk of taking his eyes off the road, to make his point, Adam turned and stared at her determinedly.

Charlene, chin canted in his direction, puckered out her lower lip. "Already, I'm fired?"

"Not really. I'm just laying out the game plan. Plain, simple, and very, very much to the point."

"Gotcha, boss man. Hey. You never worked on a plantation, did you?"

"Don't get cute. Try and remember. We are out to save a brother."

"Okay, Massuh. What next?"

This woman, without working at it much, could turn cute into unbearable.

"All right, so we've nailed down our objective. But then there's also got to be a theme. For that we can also look to Oscar, who's been singing it from the very get-go. It's his song, "Brother Where Are You?". Which in our context simply means, why still no real coming together? And that, by the way, is the gist of his own sorry plight, where but for the lack of any genuine reaching out in the entertainment industry, our guy would be not only an artistic, but also a huge financial success. In fact, I've been thinking it might be a good idea, and quite meaningful, to call the book not *Brother Where Are You*, but *Brother Where Were You*."

"Solid. That's terrific, Adam."

"Thanks. I kind of like it myself."

"You want to know something? I've always been sort of a loner. But if ever I do get to have a real close friend, I'd like it to be someone like you."

"Knock it off."

"What's the matter? You don't like compliments?"

"I find them embarrassing."

"Aha. So you're not all business, after all."

What the devil was she up to now? Or he, for that matter? It wasn't exactly more maneuvering or scheming. It was rather more like his being impelled by an odd inclination to operate on two distinctly separate levels. On the one hand he was involved with Oscar and the book, the ostensible reason for their being together on this luminous and nice smelling day. Yet at the same time he couldn't help himself from appreciating her obvious appeal. Keeping these two things separate was making for an impossible mental contortion.

But why not speak straightforwardly about both? Why

did he feel so constrained to address only the one? Why the limiter, this governor on his tongue? It was an intriguing question. She certainly didn't appear to have that kind of a problem.

"You know, I've never crossed the line."

"What's that?"

"You don't know? Gone to bed with a white guy. That's what. I did date one in college for awhile but all we ever did was neck and ride around kinda tight-like on his motorcycle. The brothers really lost their cool on catchin' us together and made me break it off."

"What's that got to do with anything?"

"C'mon now, Doc. We both of us know it's got to do with everything."

What to say? Being up front with thoughts or feelings remained for him, at best, no more than an interesting perhaps fascinating, possibility.

"You want to talk about race relations?"

"That is not quite what I was getting at."

Adam ignored the correction. He knew he'd be more comfortable with the general subject, as he'd posed it and not with where she was taking it. With Oscar's history, racial harmony was certainly a relevant ground for their discussion.

But he'd just as soon avoid any issue of out and out interracial intimacy. Particularly now that he'd been handed the image of this handsome young woman, as a precocious coed, riding through an aghast campus town in some close-clutching tandem fashion on board a motorcycle. He started thinking he could almost see her superb hands clasped around the white guy's waist.

"Well, I think that sort of thing is a chancy business

and isn't apt to change much, even if some of us do like getting on together."

"Like?"

"Or whatever. You know. Each to his own."

That was as far as he wanted to venture with the juicier subject.

"Why's that?"

"It's biological. No more than natural for people to be wary of differences. It got to be built in just because it had its survival advantages for so long. You know, during evolution."

"Baloney. I think white boys can be cute. And a lot softer."

Adam smiled.

"Thank God, I'm practically an old man."

"Looks to me like you've managed to hang in there pretty damned well. But tell me, Adam. If you're so convinced about blacks and whites can never quite stand to really come together, how you figuring to have this pitch for Oscar catch on? If I understand you right, you believe that people with the money and the power, the big time white guys, have never been able to handle his kind of message."

"That's right. But we're going to bypass them. We are going to tell a story that is to be aired in public, and it will be about this unique entertainer who may just about die without ever having gotten his due. And we will say that if that bad scene can be avoided, then millions of people will no longer be cheated out of the entertainment experience of a lifetime. If we can move that idea along, get that kind of word out, and create the demand, I'm willing to make bet that those show business moguls will forget everything except how to get into the act and have Oscar out there every which way possible. They'll be fighting over him. They'll get past all that other stuff and wind up remembering only what they really care about, making a buck on what sells."

"One other problem."

"What's that?"

"How with a mere book do you manage to get across the excitement of what's really a musical and eye-popping experience? How with words do you persuade people of a kind of magic?"

"You don't write a `mere' book. You come up with a great one. By hiring you, I hope, a damned good writer. So once we're back in town, I'll give you the tapes. I want you to listen to them carefully and think about how you're going to set about all this. Then take a first stab at it and let me look it over. Meanwhile, I'll be going over the stuff in your folder. We'll wait until I see what you've come up with before making any suggestions. Okay?"

"Right."

"We'll just have to see where we go from there."

"So It'll be like me having an audition?"

"Exactly."

"Gotcha, Adam. Gotcha."

They had come upon the gate to the marina. Ordinarily, Adam would have just been waved on through. His car was thoroughly familiar to the guards on any of the various shifts. And he had a membership sticker prominently displayed at the lower left corner of his windshield. But on this day there was no smiling wave of free passage.

"Hi there, Doctor Grossman. Great day. You picked

yourself a winner, didn't you? Gonna take her out? You know, the boat."

Adam wondered why, all of a sudden, there was this silly kind of drivel. He couldn't remember ever being held up by the gate people before.

"Hi there, miss. You know you're going out with one of our best and safest captains? Did you know that?"

The guy had bent over and was leaning toward the passenger side window. Tapping the visor of his cap at Charlene, he'd come up with an all-knowing kind of grin.

Finally catching on, Adam moved the car forward rather abruptly, passed through the gateway and headed for a parking area. Charlene was soon admiring the marina setting as they walked in the direction of his slipway.

"It's a real neat place, Adam. And you've got tremendous security here, haven't you?"

She had dug an elbow into his side, screwed up a corner of her mouth, and was winking up at him, as if to make a comedy of her overstated slyness.

"What's that supposed to mean?"

"Why, the nice man at the gate, silly. He was being so polite and protective, wasn't he?"

"Hell. Until I recognized him, I was thinking he might be someone new. He's never acted like that before."

"You really don't get it, do you?"

To the contrary, but Adam had decided to play dumb. "How's that?"

"Dirty old white married man with cute little black chick. That's what."

"I'm not dirty in the least."

"Okay. I'll take the rest as a compliment. But he sure wouldn't have ogled me like that if I were a white gal."

"C'mon, Charlene. You're being too sensitive. And besides, you're almost white."

"Yeah. Almost. But screw that little difference."

"You'd rather be white?"

"A dumb, dumb question. Forget it, Adam. Let it go. So where's your boat?"

He pointed her in the right direction leading the way along the dock. Then a new voice from over on the left.

"Hi Doc. Haven't seen you for awhile. Gonna give the young lady a sailing lesson?"

It was a dock hand checking out mooring lines. Which was usual, ordinary. What wasn't ordinary was his leering manner and how, addressing Adam, he managed to look more at Charlene.

Adam helped her on board giving no reply. Charlene was still out to needle.

"Hey Doc? You got this neat little black number here for some kind of a sailing lesson?"

"Come off it. I see what you mean."

"Why, I declare," she winked, "whatever other reason could there be for havin' this lil' ol' black bitch out here?"

Adam didn't even see it coming. He just did it because it needed doing. Leaning forward, he kissed her. Barely so, only on the forehead, with a sense of it being required of him.

"Right. It's gonna be a sailing lesson. So put on this life jacket, shut up, and we'll try and move out."

"What do I say? Will 'aye, aye sir' fit the bill?"

He checked out the marine radio, made sure various pieces of equipment like bilge pumps, knotmeter, and fathometer, were in working order, pulled off the mainsail cover, and fired up the engine. Then, mooring lines released, he slowly eased his 28 footer out of the slip and into a nearby channel leading over a short distance to the bay.

"Here. Take the wheel and head her right up into the wind while I raise the mainsail."

"Which way's that?"

"See the arrow swinging around on top the mast? That's our wind indicator. Okay? Well, just keep it pointed straight ahead in line with the boat. And steer just like you would a car."

"I'm underprivileged. Never owned or drove one."

"That bad off, huh?"

"No. Just talking silly. Anyway, I never had need of a car. I'm strictly a city girl."

"Well, to go right, just turn right and vice versa. Okay?"

"Aye, aye, sir."

Adam raised the mainsail, then taking over, set a course slightly off the wind. As the main filled and the boat began to sail, he shut the engine down. Charlene was impressed.

"Isn't it quiet though?"

"And how I like it."

"I'll stay shut up."

"That's not what I mean. It's just happens to be what I come out here for. No more than the sound of water slipping by the hull, the waves, the birds screaming at one another. I've never understood why some people drive all the way out here just to roar around in big and atrociously noisy power boats."

He tightened on the mainsheet, headed up closer to the wind, and began releasing his headsail.

"Hey, what you doing now? You're gonna flip us over."

"Relax. I'm just letting out our other sail, the jib. It gives us more power but tilts us a bit. That's what's called heeling to leeward, or away from the wind. Stay cool, kiddo. I guarantee we will not flip over and sink. There's four thousand pounds of lead ballast down below, built into the keel, and it's working full time like a pendulum to prevent that from happening."

"What will crazy old whitey think of next?"

"How do you know it wasn't some smart-assed nigger who figured it out?"

"Ain't you heard? Only sailing we ever did was on slave ships."

"You mean to tell me your great, great old gran' daddy wasn't a king and your great, great grand mammy a queen?"

"Stick it, Adam. Just stick it and shut up. So'ze you can go on and listen to your dumb waves."

"We having some kind of a fight?"

"'Course not, old man. Can't you tell?" She'd switched over to beaming at him. "I'm just having myself a wing-ding of a time. Never seen anything like this before, much less gotten to do it."

Adam was in his favored spot, backed against a cushion on his side of the cockpit and peering ahead into oncoming waves as they pressed their way past the hull. Charlene, seated across from him, had made herself comfortable by leaning against the cabin hatch and facing aft. Not much passed between them for quite awhile.

Then she almost whispered. "Hopeless, right?"

"What's that?"

"You know. Old Martin's dream of blacks and whites together."

"I'm afraid so."

"Like I said. Damned crazy old whitey."

"No. Like I said, just nature. White and black human

nature. No fault on either part but still a helluva problem. Particularly here in your good old multiracial U. S. of A."

"I still say. Crazy old whitey."

"Listen, girl. There's enough fault in it for the sharing. And if you want to pick on white racism, what do you think's going on when you light skinned blacks start ganging up on your only slightly darker brothers and sisters? I shouldn't be the one to point up your own kinds of discrimination.

"And how about your own anti-Semites and your arrogant black Muslims? And let's not forget that when a black professional lands a job in a white university, everybody genuflects and he just about gets the keys to the kingdom. He can climb to the very top of the academic ladder. White schools are even in a dead heat competing for talented blacks. But just let some altruistic white guy join the faculty of a black university and he doesn't have a prayer of a chance for advancement.

"One of the best neurologists I know was naive enough to put in twenty-five years at one of those places and instead of making him chief when it was high time for it, they did an about face and gave the job to a real dodo who, though only fresh out of school, happened to be black. He hadn't even managed to get himself certified in his field at the time he was appointed. Invariably, those institutions either pick some guy like that or they search around for some other old faithful black insider who's waiting in the wings. It's never a well-qualified white outsider. Talk about closed shops. Only time an accomplished white man is recruited at a black school is when they're in desperate need of a bailout so as to stay accredited or to latch onto some grant money they wouldn't otherwise qualify for. But then, as soon as they're started up on whatever's needed, they dump him.

"You see, to be a role model at a black school, all you have to be is some shade of black, even if you are no more than a colorful idiot. A white skinned genius, by their standards, can never be a role model. Is it a wonder that so many black schools are mediocre? It's only partly to do with limited funding. So come off this blame-it-all-on-whitey business."

"Don't look now but your prejudice is showing."

"Nope. I'm calling it right down the middle. And you want to know how else I happen to have it straight?"

"Tell me, old daddy."

"I'm not your daddy, old or young."

"Not even my sweet old sugar daddy?"

"Especially not your sugar daddy. You stand to get no more than an honest day's pay for an honest day's work, plus a percentage if we make out."

"If we what?"

"Sorry. If we succeed. I misspoke. But back to what I was saying. I know how right I am because I got the exact same word from the man himself, from Oscar."

"What's he know about any of that?"

"Well, when he was at Brandon University as an artist-in-residence, and was knocking himself out, trying to mount student performances that were worthwhile, he observed just what I'm talking about. There's a school with the worst damned closed academic shop you'll find anywhere. Oscar used to watch them pocket every cent they could squeeze out of the federal government and then go and squander it. Somehow they'd managed to latch onto whatever tax money Congress had voted for their support, then go ahead and use it to hire more administrators than any other college of comparable size and to finance half million dollar retirement packages for highly placed insiders. Naturally they'd run scared of suggestions to streamline or to innovate any changes that were needed. And the last thing in the world they'd want to have to deal with would be someone truly creative. Someone like Oscar. Someone who makes artistic waves. More so, of course, if the person's white, but even if like him, they turn out being black.

"That bunch is terrified by anyone wanting to do things better. You can ask Oscar about that kind of prejudice. Those incompetent blacks out there are running so scared of having their shortcomings and their greedy grabbings exposed that they're ready to discriminate against anyone who might conceivably rock their precious little stalled boat. Oscar couldn't accomplish a damned thing for the entire two years he put in with them. Hell girl. As bad as it may be in the streets, Oscar accomplished a damned sight more in the streets, working with ghetto toughs, than with college kids in that narrow-minded, supposedly nurturing, but really stifling black academic community. But you know, it's the same the world over. So don't blame it all on whitey. There's no color line whatever for lazy, self promoting, incompetence."

Adam wondered what he was really getting so steamed up about.

"I'm beginning to get it, Adam. You don't like whites or blacks, do you? What you into? Chinkies?"

"Atoms, girl. Just give me a dumb old atom, anytime. Or a quark, maybe. And if you can't manage that, I'll take any old beat up electron. But deliver me from the human race. They're plain and simple, a nutty bunch. And skin color is the least part of it."

"Is that why you need so much time for yourself? Why you're looking to hire me for all this writing?"

"Well. In a way."

"So you're into lab work now?"

"Not really. I wouldn't know a spectrometer if I fell across it. What I need time for is to sort a few things out. It's important for guys my age."

"That's news to me. All the old guys I run into are only looking to get it up and on, maybe one more time. Sure you don't just need to get laid?"

She leaned across the cockpit in his direction. Forearms folded across her thighs, she seemed to be searching his face for some indication of such a hankering. Why was everybody so set on getting him laid?

"No."

"No? Just like that, a no?"

"When you're sure, you're sure. C'mon, let's do some sailing."

"Shit. How can we avoid it? This boat thing's got a mind of its own. Doesn't it though? Is there a way to stop it, Adam? That's if you had to? Has it got, like brakes?"

"No. What you have to do is furl, that means wind up the sails, or drop them, or just release them briefly so as to spill the wind out of them. You know, it's like when they say, `the wind went out of his sails'. Or you can head straight up into the wind and sort of flutter out and stall. Of course, no matter what you do, you're gonna drift a ways. And even if you turn the engine back on and go quickly into reverse, because of your momentum, there's always a certain amount of forward motion that can't be checked. The point being that if you do find yourself heading for some kind of a collision, changing course is a much better option than trying to stop."

"No real turning back, hey Adam?"

"I'm afraid not. It's all a matter of trying to limit the consequences or the damages, for something you've started and are committed to, however you want to look at it. You know. As in all things."

"What in hell we talking about, Adam? This damned boat? Life? You and me? You wouldn't happen to have an idea, would you? All I did was ask you where the brakes were on this fool thing. You always been like this? Complicated and far out? And like you've resigned yourself to something awful?"

"No. Actually, it started up the other night while I was listening to the radio."

"Gotta' watch that stuff. It can blow your mind. What was it? One of those evangelical stations? Some of those guys are real weirdos."

"No. Just a late night interview. Why don't we drop all this? I'd rather concentrate on sailing."

Adam turned again to his waves, but Charlene ignored his suggestion.

"So it's not about religion. You're not religious. Is that right?"

"Right. Except about my sailing, when I'm sailing. Get it?"

This was a very persistent gal. Adam hoped she'd be as dogged about her writing effort.

"I always thought that every Jew was at least a little religious. Aren't you supposed to be the chosen people?"

"Chosen for what?"

"Why, to lead the rest of us out of this mess."

"It's not a mess. We're just not going anywhere. We're going round and round. Then down."

"And no one's watching?"

"Probably not."

"But it might just pay to be one of the good guys, anyway?"

"Maybe so. If you want to stake everything on heavenly rewards. That sort of thing has always turned me off."

"Why's that?"

"Well I just can't imagine anything better than life itself. And for my money the religionists strike me as being spoilers. Fear of dying has them groveling and just about begging for what's not to be had. Worse than that, it's turned a lot of them, the so-called believers, into an evangelical horde of life denigrators. They'd just about deny us what little reason we have for breathing."

"But suppose you're wrong."

"I come out here for a simple sail, and maybe a business discussion, and wind up covering the philosophical waterfront. Okay. So you want an out? Ever hear of Pascal's wager?"

"Nope."

"Well, Pascal didn't quite believe, but figured there'd be nothing lost in being one of your so-called good guys. So he hedged his bet."

"But you do have something to lose. That way you don't ever get to really live it up, to the utmost. You're neither here nor there."

"Right. If that's what you're into, you don't. Apparently, Pascal had other things on his mind than living it up."

"You know? That's what really sends me about being a

writer. A writer might have something like that, something like what we've been talking about, or what Pascal had to say, something special, and there it'd be. Once you get it down in print, it's there to be read about, forever and ever."

No need to set her straight on that score. Better to hold his tongue. Should she react, as he had, to the quite contrary reality, he stood to lose himself a potentially indispensable helpmate.

"Got to make your mark, hey Charlene?"

"Yeah man."

"Good. But remember, with *Brother Where Were You*, we do not have to be knocking ourselves out for something eternally true or especially remarkable. Our sights are set quite a bit lower. All we're looking for is a quick literary fix, a tad of instant notoriety for our boy."

She pleaded playfully.

"I can't slip in a little something for myself?"

"Oh sure. But remember why we're doing this. We need to keep our eye on the ball."

Charlene signaled her understanding with a nod and saying no more, reclined a bit against the cabin hatch. After awhile, under influence of the boat's motion, she began to nod, finally finding it more comfortable to slide down fully and sprawl across the cushions on her side of the cockpit. Soon she was asleep. Now, when Adam was not staring across or into the oncoming water, he could finally study her uninterruptedly.

Dressed as she was in tight fitting designer jeans and T-shirt, there was no problem in convincing himself that Charlene's body was perfectly turned out. His gaze shifted from that bountiful form to a seductively inviting mouth.

It was typically full lipped, and half agape, making show of a disconcertingly provocative tongue. .

Were there no other considerations, what recourse would he have but to drop sail and ask her below? Hard as it was to forego such fancy, he must stick with his original plan. This had to be a serious arrangement. If wishful longings did insist on intruding, Oscar's needs must still come first. Always, there was Oscar. So he let her sleep, yet was set on wondering, why all of a sudden, for the very first time, he'd become so ready to stray.

Later, when she awakened, they sailed for another hour during which he explained the basic aerodynamic principles of sailing, tacking, jibing, and running on the wind. Through it all he had the distinct feeling of being not only listened to but of himself being once again intently scrutinized. It'd become her turn in a game they were both playing.

On the trip back into Washington, she quizzed him a lot more about Oscar, but when they were a few blocks away from her apartment building, the subject changed.

"Now Adam, you don't have some kind of a serious illness, do you?"

"Hell no. Why do you ask?"

"Well, all this business about it being a last chance to do something for Oscar has me wondering if maybe it's not Oscar's last chance but yours we are dealing with. The way you carry on, a person might think you were already half dead."

"I'm A-okay. I can assure you."

"Well good. Besides, from the practical standpoint, I don't want to start on something you won't be around to finish."

Smiling, she jabbed him in the ribs again good naturedly.

Once he'd pulled over to the curb in front of her building Charlene got out and waited as he went around to the trunk for his package containing Oscar's recordings and career summary. He handed them over to her sounding and looking his usual steadfast self.

"All right. Here you go. Enjoy. But be sure and take it in carefully. He's had one helluva life and much of it is right here. It's up to you to turn it into one..."

Charlene had the package in hand, but taking him by surprise, she'd encircled his neck with her other arm drawing him tightly to her, and interrupting his admonition. No woman, particularly one kissing him for the first time, had ever done it so open-mouthed and with that much tongue. He couldn't help but engulf her in return, but just as quickly, she'd broken away and laughing, put some distance between them. Soon she was calling back at him tauntingly.

"Just so's I know you ain't dead yet, white boy. Can't afford to lose you. Now beat it on home and change your drawers."

Ten

Oscar had been in California for six days. Adam's only contacts with Charlene were by telephone. She was listening to tapes and becoming increasingly enthusiastic. Had never heard anyone who "knocked her out" the way Oscar did.

Clare, apprised of this new situation, wanted no part of it. She had decided that Charlene was bad news.

"You know nothing about this woman. And anyway, what point is there in it? Right now the last thing in the world you need is more free time. Free time, which as far as I can see, you just spend around here moping. You sit around and stare at absolutely nothing, or even worse, you watch the tube. Why not at least take a stab at writing it yourself? If it doesn't work out, there's always time to hire someone."

"We don't have a lot of time."

"You going somewhere?"

"No. But are you all of a sudden forgetting what this is all about? Oscar's pressing situation? That's what. Hell, less than a week ago you were having an absolute fit about how we needed to get going post haste."

"You're right. But I didn't mean to run right out and hire the first floozy to come along."

"I see. I can't hire someone who might be a floozy to simply do a little writing for us, but it's perfectly all right to jump in the sack with any old gal who'd probably be just that? C'mon, Clare. Start making sense."

"Is that it, Adam? You're killing two birds with the same stone? Well. Thank you very much. I must really be getting stupid in my old age. You know it never occurred to me. But if that's what you're up to, I'm even more opposed."

"Please. Spare me any more of this. She is just a writer."

"It's basic. You do not mix business with pleasure. And you certainly also do not..."

"Clare. Especially spare me the rest of that one. And believe me. I am getting absolutely no satisfaction out of any of this. To the contrary."

"Maybe so far you haven't."

And that, apparently only for the time being, was that. She stomped off.

Wouldn't it be nice, he thought, to do away with phones? Because Oscar was at him next, all the way from Los Angeles.

"I'm stayin' put out here a few more days. Meetin' up with some civic leaders in Watts. Also been talkin' to Jesse Jackson and a certain congresswoman. So what's happenin' with you? Any word from that chick? You know, your so-called writer."

"Don't you start up on me. Now I've also got Clare sticking it to me and royally. She's flat-out opposed to Charlene."

"Yeah? Well maybe you ought to listen to your old

lady. That woman is on to everything. She knows exactly where she and most other people are comin' from. You remember, years ago, how when all of us were in New York, and over on the west side at that crazy townhouse of Miles? Remember how he peeled an orange and started passin' out slices off the tip of that long and nasty lookin' kitchen knife of his so we'd each of us get a taste?"

"Can't say I do. All I remember is the palm trees and that crazy monkey in the bathroom. But what the hell has that got to do with anything we're talking about?"

"Yeah. Well, what you should have noticed was that even though he and that young wife of his were married only one damn week, all he wanted to do was talk to Clare. He told me a little later on that he'd never met a woman with so such smarts and all that cool. Maybe you don't know it but you have lucked out well enough to have yourself a real hip woman, a winner. But you are not payin' any attention to her. Wise up, man. Do whatever Clare tells you."

"You about through?"

"Hell no. You haven't answered me. What's that chick doin'?"

"She's listening to the tapes. Says you knock her out."

"That's great. Now all we need is the next contender. Did you happen to tell her this is not the fight business? It is show business we are presently into?"

"Funny you should say that. Now let's see how good your own memory might be. That show of yours, *Big Time Buck White*. You know, the one that folded in New York after only a one week run? Remember it?"

"How in hell could I ever forget? Someone said the

promoters conned us into doin' that show only so they could pull out with an investment loss. They were just about wettin' their pants for us to flop for tax purposes. Those fuckers actually handed us our closin' notices on openin' night, even though they had Muhammad Ali playing the lead role. How about that? A'course I don't know it for certain. It was just a rumor and we did get some word from them later on about takin' the show to New York, but nothin' ever came of it."

"Yeah? Well see if you can remember what one opening night reviewer put in his column the next day just because he happened to spot the heavyweight champ and some of his buddies sitting up front in the orchestra and yakking it up."

"Damned if I do."

"Well, let me help you. What he said was that your show couldn't really amount to very much because look who was sittin' there and applauding. Suggesting that if only some dumb fight palookas were the ones to dig it, it wasn't worth bothering to take in. And saying nothing about all the cheers you got come curtain time from what happened to be a packed house."

"So what? What's the connection?"

"Nothing much. Just something I recall because of you wanting me to remind Charlene we are not in the fight business. Seems there was a time that at least one biased reviewer, getting on your case, thought you were. Suggesting that you'd better make your pitch to other than a dumb fight crowd if you ever wanted to make it in show business."

"Well, as you know very well, he didn't know what the fuck he was talkin' about. That was a great show. People still dig it every time I put it on. Didn't you even record it for the two runs we had in that Atlanta church a few years back?"

"Right."

"You tryin' to change the subject? Which is your new little friend, how far she's gotten with the book, and do I assume that friends is still all you are?"

"Oscar, give me a break. She has to get tooled up and in a creative mood. It's not as if she knows your material the way I do. Hold your water a little while longer and try to understand. We are not doing straight biography. This book has to do something different, something special. It has to make exactly the right kinda pitch, find a special groove, and that takes some explaining on my part and planning on hers. But she'll be settling down to it. And from the samples of her writing that I've looked at, she's got what it takes."

"What else you samplin', Adam? I can just see you and her, real relaxed like, spinnin' records, listenin' to our tapes, and gettin' yourselves in, like you say, some groovy kinda' mood. But what you two are probably plannin' ain't got nothin' to do with business, man. Remember? Business. And we are not into mood music, Adam. Never have and never will be. So it's high time for action and let me tell you once more, in case it still needs emphasizin', it's writin' action I am speakin' of. Lawd a mercy. These women. What I go through. They will surely be my end."

"I've got the message. We will try to expedite things."

"Not things, Adam. Expedite your damned chick to start writin'. Move her along."

Their conversation needed redirection.

"Now actually. What are you up to out there?"

"Mostly meetin' with school kids. Tryin' to inspire them to get somewhere with their lives. But you know, other than bustin' into places, what is there really for them these days? They are just not being given any chances for somethin' else. I'm poppin' music at them. It's the only kinda' fix I know. But it's still no alternative to muggin' someone when your stomach's empty and you ain't trained in any way. Man, it's rough out here. These kids in Watts are close on to runnin' wild. And drugs? Hell. Some of these so-called black leaders are as ridiculous as the white clowns with their `just-say-no' kinda' shit. They've got nothin' to offer on that score either. No one out here is the least bit savvy on how to keep these kids from becomin' hardened criminals. What is really necessary is some kinda' innovation that has down to earth promise. You can't just do stupid things like talkin' to them about paintin' garbage trucks or cleanin' up the sidewalks. They gotta get into somethin' real. Of course, as far as music goes, not everyone can get to star or be leadin', but like I tell 'em, some could do the advertisin' or other useful things."

"You aren't sounding off to the media, are you?"

"It's not like reporters have a way of fallin' all over me these days. Now do they Adam? Best you can remember?"

"No. But this is different. From what I'm hearing from you this is about some kind of a riot that might just happen. And you can not afford to be in the thick of it. You do that, and all the promoting in the world isn't going to help any. When's it going to dawn on you that you can't have it both ways? On the one hand you want to be performing and on the other you simply have to get yourself into all this other stuff which turns certain people off. How about cooling it for awhile? At least until you've stashed away some money? Then, when you've got it made, you can afford to be political. All we need right now is for some TV crew to catch you acting up on some fool street corner."

"Later on is just too fuckin' late for these kids, Adam. They are out of time. And the street is where they're at, so that's where I am also. They don't have any other place. Where else you expectin' somebody to find them and to help out?"

"Now you know damned well it won't work, so why spin your wheels? You need reminding what happened in Atlanta?"

In the mid-60s, Oscar got himself involved with that city's most notorious gang, the Mighty East Side Outlaws. He was doing a show in Atlanta, but because of all the Outlaws' rumbling and what not, people didn't feel safe about going to the theater. He decided to seek the Outlaws out but they wouldn't meet up with him.

Finally he tracked down a hundred or so in an abandoned building. They were "lookin' like a herd of pissed off bulls". Oscar told them they were "killin' his action", "waylayin" his audience. He offered to let them put on their own show which he'd direct. It came off. And that show, employing a dozen gang members, went on in a church. Oscar had kept telling these kids that if they would cut out their gangstering and do something straight, something like this, everything would be cool.

But it didn't turn out that way at all. The project received little civic or press attention. No one, it seemed, wanted to endorse a bunch of hoodlums. And there was no public support. The result being that Oscar came away announcing, for all to hear, that the cops simply wanted the gangs to stay the way they were so they could beat up on them.

Oscar, reminded of what had gone on in Atlanta, started to get a little hot under his L.A. collar.

"Adam, you have a one-track mind. Say what you will, it did not just stop there. So things didn't work out in Atlanta. So what? You win some. You lose some. From that situation, I latched onto better ideas. Don't be forgettin' the talent shows I staged in Ohio. And you know who got started there? Hell man. We gave first prize to the Dreamers. We damned well discovered those cats and started them off. Way back in '71. And we've been able to work with school kids findin' themselves in a jam all around this country. I've been able to send a message of Afro self-esteem and of our noble history to a helluva lot 'a places. Just crazy damn places. And look how all that inspired me to do black poetry and those hip TV shows on public television. You know something, man? I'd just love to start workin' with some of them real mean gangs out here, like the Dudes or the Rappers. We'd have them doin' terrific things other than riotin'."

"You don't happen to have any more gigs out there, do you?"

"Just one. A small club outside of town. It's no big deal."

"Now look here, Oscar. Any gig right now is a very big deal. So try and remember this. The streets are a separate thing. If you have to be in them, for Christ's sake try and stay out of trouble. And on this club date, can't you just, for now, stick with being upbeat? Even slaphappy wouldn't hurt any. It'd go a long way. The audience, believe me on this, the audience just wants to have a good time. Right now, they do not want to hear how it is `out there in the streets, baby.' They are just looking for a few precious detached moments in which to forget all of that stuff. So how about doing what you do better than anyone else? Make 'em laugh. Have them rocking in their seats. Get them roaring. Get them jumping in the aisles. And stamping their feet for more of the same. You do what you can like that out there and we will go to work in our own little grinding way back here. Like you've been saying, just about ad nauseum. It's maybe the one last chance we have for hitting pay dirt. So don't, at this late stage of the game, start messing up."

"Yeah, I dig it. But you know something? All those clappin' hands are just fine, but when the clappin' and the screamin' is over and done with, and everybody's gone home, it doesn't wind up meanin' a fuckin' thing. You are back bein' alone, man. There is nobody but you. And that's when you have to face up to what it is that's really on your mind and really important. And in my mind it's what life's turned out to be for black people out there in those streets you want me to forget about. You think on it, Adam, next time you see me doin' even one of those so-called upbeat numbers you're so partial to. You look a little more closely and you might just finally get to seein', and to understandin', that in those same songs there's a sneaky old current of sad-assed truth, the sad, black kind of truth. It's there in all my stuff even when the audience is havin' such a good old time."

"So what in hell are we trying to sell with this book of ours? What's everybody supposed to have been doing without, been deprived of? Not outstanding melody? Not great lyrics bordering on poetry? Not happy times as well as poignant moments? What the devil are we trying to package off? Is it not that? Or is it rather Oscar Brown Jr., our own little, finally-out-of-the-closet Che Guevarra?"

"Hey man. I like that. I like it. That's what I call bein' creative."

"You've got to be kidding."

"No. That's something to be workin' on."

"In the book?"

"No. You crazy, man? A new number, man. A new number. Me and Che. Che, Che, Che. Gotta go now. Dinner's cookin'."

Yes, thought Adam, who but a crazy man would get himself into such a fix? How could a newly retired chest surgeon take on the obligation of getting out a winner of a book on a hip, show biz genius determined, absolutely determined, to make himself in the mind of anyone with a say in the matter, utter box office poison?

However substantial the talent of his friend, the proposition was truly daunting for other reasons. For example, how does one write in any attractive context that Oscar, the guy who once tried running for the state legislature, had also been a communist? Or how does one skip casually by his flagrantly daring and open use of marijuana?

And was it conceivable that somewhere out there existed lots of potentially sympathetic ears for news that Oscar had not filed a federal income tax return in twenty years? That after reading the constitution, he had irrevocably concluded, and it was his considered legal opinion, there was no legitimate basis for taxing black Americans because they had never had any say in the matter of being brought here?

Just as well the ball was now in Charlene's corner.

Eleven

He needed time for himself. Each of them had their "thing." Clare could take to puttering about the house, her various books and her friends. Oscar, assuredly, wherever he was, would be in the thick of something or other. And Charlene was presumably listening to tapes while getting tooled up for their joint project. They had their choosings. He must have his own. And that was to make sense, not only of this entire business with Oscar, but how did it figure in the larger order of his new and foreboding mindset? Plus, there was the fact that the assumed role of schemer was starting to get him down.

The promotion of Oscar's career, when looked at from his new perspective, looked like a complete waste of time. However his days might be spent in that role, they'd be squandered. The effort might serve Oscar well enough but what was really to be gained from it all, any more than from any other endeavor, in a universe ultimately defeating of every purpose?

All enterprise had become meaningless and there was no way around that certainty. This being a given, how could time be thought of as anything other than moments dumbly suffered or pleasured through? How could one apply it to anything? Much less a slight book in a world of absolute insubstantiality. This cast of mind had an obsessive hold upon him.

But was there really some possibility of quitting? Was he not, just like everyone, an ensnared biological automaton driven by unfathomable urging? Getting things done for no better reason than their doing was transparently foolish but still the insistent way of all flesh, including his own, even as it headed towards the flame.

So it looked as though life had him along on one more of its silly and useless rides, there being no turning back. Somehow, he must resign himself to what stood to be just another futile action.

Adam's difficulty went beyond the forfeiture of a future. He'd also been cheated of that satisfaction ordinarily drawn from his own past achievements, voiding the possibility of making any kind of permanently estimable mark. Existence and all of its works were to become so much amorphous, worthless, smoke.

The more he thought about it, the more he appreciated how much he'd structured his life to make such a mark. It was what had kept him going professionally, made him write scientific articles, driven him to document his clinical innovations. Well then, if all of that was now to be denied him, where might he find that other kind of pleasure, the kind he'd only sampled so briefly before the fateful night of that radio broadcast?

Pleasure certainly had no life of its own, unless you were into chemicals or something of that sort. Otherwise, it needed to be derived. But right now he hadn't a prayer, not a chance of evoking it. Alcohol, drugs, stuff like that... they were out of the question. And so far, his earlier presumptions about finding pleasure in what was terminal had amounted to no more than unrealized speculation.

Which brought about, for a brief consideration, the question of interventional, hopeful prayer. Adam had no imbued much less an adopted familiarity with it. As he'd always been quick to tell people, Charlene being his most recent audience, that any taste for such life-deriding mumbo-jumbo was utterly beyond him. His lifetime focus had been on making his mark among the assemblages of atoms, not among the angels. So now, if out of sheer desperation he must turn to some kind of high and mighty one and only for a sense of well being, or even just for solace, he had no way out by way of the ethereal world, either.

He did not doubt that Clare was quite correct in her suggestion of pleasure being accessible to other people by dint of what might be his own good works in their behalf. And he'd have no argument with this effort in Oscar's interest--which Adam saw as no more than the discharge of an obligation--assuring at the very least, brief pleasure to Oscar, and probably also satisfaction to Clare.

But what about himself? The prospect of doing good didn't seem to be setting off any particularly pleasant vibrations. Maybe it was supposed to, but it surely wasn't. If ever he'd had the ability, it had gotten out of kilter by now.

What might be done, to relieve his growing unease and the bleak possibility he'd never again find satisfaction in anything? Left to pondering that sad predicament, he turned to what medical knowledge he possessed for answers. But was this not the very definition of depression?

Depression being, just as he'd describe his own state, the inability to experience pleasure? So short of potent antidepressant drugs, did science have any suggestions for him, of a possible way out?

Considering it from that scientific point of view (Adam's main strength), he recalled that there were behavioral ways consistently described as being linked to pleasure. It had all to do with evolution and survival. For example, vigorous exercise and one upsmanship in battle or in surrogate sporting activities, were well known as favored options. Agreeable food was predictably pleasurable. The act of self-cleansing would also press a favorable button.

But he'd no yen for either strenuous exercise or conflict. And to become a fat gourmet, or to immerse himself the day long in some hot tub, was utterly out of the question.

So, looking for answers, he searched the uncaring sky, prowled for hours over hiking trails in Rock Creek Park alongside his panting wolfhound, and listened to all kinds of music. He did begin to quicken his pace a bit, even around the house, remembering that someone had once said that by doing no more than walking slightly faster would release endorphin molecules into the blood stream and could be counted on to be mood elevating. Whoever that guy was, he didn't know what he was talking about because it didn't work. Nor did anything else.

Thus far, what was left, he'd considered off limits.

After a few days, he called to check on Charlene's progress.

"How's it going?"

"Well. Not bad at all. I'm finished with the tapes of his recordings. Which means, I suppose, that I've listened to just about everything Oscar's done on records. But didn't you say something about also having made a few live recordings?"

"Right. I taped some stage shows, and performances in clubs, including a good one right here in Washington at Blues Alley. There's one number I'm especially fond of. He sings up a storm and pledges an intriguing number of things, all very sexy."

"When do I get to hear all that?"

"Anytime you like. I've got some extra copies."

"Can you run them by?"

"Tomorrow afternoon?"

"Sure. That'd be fine."

"Okay, no problem. How's two o'clock?"

"See you then. I'm in 5C. Just ring from downstairs and I'll buzz you through."

No sooner than he'd set up this arrangement, Adam felt compromised. Never in his married life had he ever gone to some single woman's apartment. And once in his car, it was not possible but to dwell on the manner of his parting from Charlene, just a couple of days before.

With first sight of her in the open doorway there was an agitated excitement centering somewhere at the back of his knees. Without effort, he had an instant remembrance of her devilish tongue.

Inside the apartment, he noticed certain scents, different from those he'd encountered when alongside her at the theater, in his car, or on his boat.

Looking about him, he was struck by how neat and sparsely furnished was this single bedroom apartment. It was certainly a far cry from the thirty-year accumulated dust and clutter of his own house.

In what he took to be the living room she'd placed a

solitary butcher's block table on which rested her computer and a printer. There was a director's type chair nearby and another just like it against the opposite wall. A leather couch in the middle of the room. No rugs anywhere. And set on the bare floor against a side wall, a stereo. Window blinds but no curtains.

Glancing into her bedroom, Adam spotted not a bed but a tightly sheeted mattress resting directly on the floor. That was it. Other than Charlene, nothing else visible.

"I know just what you're thinking. I'm fixed up kind of simple like, but that's how I want it. Can't stand having a lot of stuff around. It's too distracting for my work. Anyways, nothing you see here, save for the stereo, actually belongs to me. It's all been rented. Even the computer's borrowed. There's absolutely nothing in this place that can bug me or that's got some kinda hold on me."

Not being offered a place to sit down, Adam walked over to a window and stared down into the street five floors below. It was empty, non-revealing.

"You know. I never got to ask where you're from. Oh... here's the material you gave me to look over. I was real impressed. I passed the word on to Oscar. And here's the tapes you asked for."

It had come out so awkwardly. Right away, she set to needling him for it.

"You about done with your check list, Adam? Recited your little say? And gettin' ready to light on outa' here?"

All accompanied by one of her all-knowing grins.

"Not really. What do you mean?"

"Okay. We'll drop it. Besides. You really want to hear about me or you simply making conversation?"

"I wouldn't do that."

"Well. I was born in Missouri and went to school in Texas. Matter of fact, I graduated from Baylor. Then I worked for awhile in Denver."

"You really got around, hey?"

"I dunno. Just went where there was a scholarship or an opening. Lots of kids, the rich ones, they get to go wherever they want. I had no such luxury. Also, I had to put myself through school waitin' on tables. Never knew my old man. Mom's a nurse, and all together there were five of us. Like they say, nothin' but a poor black girl."

"You're really not very black."

"Are you at it again? Come off it. I get that kinda stuff all the time. How colored I am has nothin' to do with it. I'm built black, 'case you haven't noticed. Besides which, you ain't even seen my butt as yet. Once you have yourself a look at that you will know exactly where I'm from. We all got something quite special back there, no matter how light or dark the Lord made us."

Adam chose not to comment on her reference to that particular body part, although whatever she might think, it had hardly escaped his notice.

"Who's that again? The Lord? That's right. You are a Baptist, aren't you?"

"And a dyed-in-the-wool, southern-style one too. That's the damned truth."

"They especially moral and all that sort of thing?"

"That's how we all talk. But not so's you'd notice from how we carry on."

Adam finally got seated on the couch. Charlene took to the tableside director's chair in which she leaned back, assuming a slouched position. She was in shorts with bare legs crossed and her hands clasped above her head. It was the kind of posture that might conceivably be struck in a manner consistent with these inquiring kinds of interchange, but that effect was defeated by the way it also happened to thrust her full breasts forward in his direction. Adam's mouth had become quite dry.

There were a few awkward moments in which he wondered what next to say. But she spared him from it.

"Adam?"

"Yes?"

"When in hell you plan on gettin' round to doin' me?"

He swallowed hard. Actually, he couldn't swallow. He could only try. It was too much in a knot back there. In part because of what she'd just said. But also because, unabashedly, she was now undressing in front of him.

Charlene drew him up from the couch. Again there was that tongue. And behind her, on the floor, in the other room, he could see the mattress. What alternative had he?

Twelve

Adam's flair for organization was soon in place, and their get-togethers became part of a set schedule. It was a good deal better than having to take some antidepressant drug once or twice daily. From what he knew of such medications, they could be associated with frequent, persistent, and even serious side effects.

Not that his more physiological kind of mood elevation was free of troubling consequences, but at least those downsides were neither persistent nor serious. Notable among them were his occasional nightmares about being found out and recurrent but transient guilt feelings.

He had never strayed like this. For the most part he'd always taken it for granted that marital fidelity would see him through to the end. Getting a handle on it analytically, however, it seemed that the betrayal of an ineffable trust was not what forced him to brood every so often.

He was certain that once you start down such a road, the perfection of the marital condition becomes destroyed forever. There's no putting it back together again. A pity too, because no oncoming starry explosion could ever have undone a lifetime untarnished relationship, if only he'd held on and kept it that way. Relationships, after all, had no firmament.

But then again, since the ultimate destruction of everything else was exactly what he must face up to, perhaps the sundering of his impeccable marital circumstance was a reasonable first step of surrender to the much more considerable inevitable. It could be a way of resigning himself to what was yet to come.

Otherwise, when not pursuing these cosmic kinds of meditation, he read novels or medical journals, had chats with Clare on political and family matters, and kept his household running. He remained, for the most part, a well-oiled, private kind of person.

He did happen to wonder, on one occasion, if things would have turned out differently if Clare and he had ever had children. Would he have been spared some of this present philosophical turmoil?

That question brought to mind a time some years before, when he'd pressed the importance of making one's mark upon a woman of academic stripe from Trinity College in Ireland. Oh, but didn't she have right at him for saying so? Declared it was so much rot, further insisting that the only way to make one's mark was not by personal achievements, but rather by having offspring. That procreation was all there was to it.

Taking that concept into consideration, Adam took to looking about him, especially in the direction of his not too stunningly achieving nephews and nieces. The prospect of that kind of progeny providing what he'd want to leave behind was altogether dismal. Better to be spared any chance of association with such a memento.

So the issue of children was already, long ago, well

addressed. At least from that standpoint. And anyway, the Irish lady had equally bizarre thoughts on why some people were creative, yet others were not. It was merely a matter of their not being able to keep themselves from being so. As simple and as far fetched as that.

Actually, his present musings about children did come down to a more practical thought. Maybe a bunch of children, scattered all over the place, merely by their distracting presence, would have softened the impact of his fateful late night astrophysical revelation and the tortured mental meanderings which followed.

But none of that had much of a real point. For unestablished reasons that Clare and he had never bothered to trouble themselves over, their destiny was not to have children. For worse rather than for better, the more he thought about it, this destiny of his was looking more and more like an all 'round killer. Even though, for the time being, it was forcing him to seek diversion.

The arrangement with Charlene was in certain respects peculiar. When they were on the telephone, they talked incessantly about Oscar. When together, he was scarcely mentioned, although often they did lounge around with his music playing softly in the background. The construction they put upon this was the possibility of furthering their thoughts regarding the book. Otherwise, they were in it for pleasure.

It could not fail to cross Adam's mind how furious Oscar would be should he learn that this was how they were carrying on. Talk about travesty. Were he to know that instead of being hard at work, they were loving it up to his words and music, there'd be all hell to pay.

As for the telephone discussions, they consisted of wide-ranging considerations on how best to approach their subject and readings by her to him of tentative passages.

Often, he would give advice on how to change a word or two, or describe events in Oscar's personal life at the time of a particular lyric. After all, who else would know that when Oscar wrote certain heart-felt lines, he was being rocked himself by the consequences of a comparable experience? Meanwhile, Clare continued to render her opinions regarding this liaison.

"Instead of you two keeping our phone all tied up, why don't you get yourself a separate line, or better still, you could just move in together."

"You want her to come over here?"

"That is not what I had in mind."

"This is great. Really great. You and Oscar are both down on this woman, yet neither one of you has ever met her. Or prepared to do the job she's taken on."

"Oh? You didn't tell me Oscar was also set against it."

"You think you've got the market cornered on paranoia?"

"And what's all this about it being some kind of a job? You aren't planning to pay her out of your own pocket, are you? I sure hope not. And I know damned well that Oscar's got no money for anything like that."

"Well, she's certainly entitled to a conventional percentage and at least, I should think, some kind of a small advance."

"I see. And how will it be figured up? Will the arrangement be, like they say in the islands, by de jahb, mahn, or will it be by de hour, mahn?"

"You're getting to be a real card in your senior years, Clare. You know that?"

"No answer. Hey, Adam? Well, she probably wants her commission figured by de hour because from where I'm sitting there's no sign yet, as far as I can tell, of any part of de jahb. Contradict me if I'm wrong. All there's been so far are hours and hours of, shall we say, everloving talk, talk, talk. Am I right or wrong?"

He didn't care very much for the barbed aspersion. It hit too close to the mark.

"Gotta' go now."

"Just whoa there, buster. That brings up another little item I've been meaning to raise. Where are you disappearing to almost every morning around this time?"

He was ready for that one having wondered when it would finally find expression.

"Clare, when all's said and done, I just couldn't stay away. I had to get back to the hospital. You know, take in a conference or two, talk to some of the residents I had a hand in training, grab coffee and a sandwich with guys in the department."

"Really? Well good for you. But be careful today, Adam. It's been raining awfully hard. And don't forget your umbrella."

Lying was the only way. He didn't want to, or like to, but again, it was a situation leaving him no alternative, because mornings were when he must head for Charlene's apartment.

Fifteen minutes later she was buzzing him in, and after a short while, life wasn't half-bad. He might even be inclined to say that in spite of everything, it was somewhat better than half good. But no more than briefly. Just like with any other antidepressant, the effects of this one were starting to wear thin.

Two PM. Still raining and time to be getting home. Charlene was beside him on the mattress and both of them were somberly eyeing the window glass obscured by watery streamings. From out the stereo in the next room Oscar was singing an equally dreary song.

Adam was feeling the kind of letdown that had started to take hold in the winding down of these dalliances and was becoming more and more insistent. Today, it wasn't helping any that the world outside their little cubicle seemed so dull. And think what he might about the importance of dealing with a situation one way or another, things still didn't usually turn out either black or white. It was somewhere in between...as grey. If he had any doubt about that, all he needed was to consider the present glum result of a simple and well-meaning idea, the delegated writing of this infernal book.

Instead of reminding him as usual of the hour, Charlene sounded a different note.

"I've got something to say and I don't want you getting all uptight about it."

For Adam, that kind of lead-in guaranteed it would happen. Why did people have to get off on bad news this way? Where did they get the cockeyed notion that anxiety could be staved off by the advance announcement of an oncoming disaster or even that being forewarned could make it easier to handle? And least of all were they being considerate. What they were being was cowardly. Afraid to come right out with the heavy stuff. Adam preferred direct, up front, declarations of any kind of deterioration, be they personal, clinical, whatever.

"C'mon, Charlene. Just spill it. Spit it out. You want to know where this relationship is going. Right?"

He had been sure that eventually there'd be questions for him, and at home as well.

"You nuts? Listen honey. There's no way in hell I'd be talking dumb like that. So I've finally crossed the line. So what? Be real, man. What we've got here is for the moment. Just for the moment. It is set to go nowhere."

That was nice. He started to feel a little better. The lovely girl beside him on their mattress had made herself a bit more lovable. Also, it seemed that she had exactly the right handle, on the nature of their conjoining.

"Charlene, you are a real adult lady."

"Yeah, and with some real adult worries. I gotta hit on you for some bread."

"Well sure. Why not? I was thinking about an advance for you only this morning. It was Clare, in fact, who brought it up. How about five hundred? Would that do you for awhile?"

How could he do that? Both to Clare, and the truth. Was he, by now, so deep into this lying business, he'd be reckless and flaunt it?

"Five hundred will not cut it at all. I need like five thousand and by the end of next week or I'm in one helluva' jam."

"You gotta' be kidding."

"I am not kidding. What I am is flat broke. My credit cards are all cancelled out and right now I owe more than three grand on my Visa alone. Besides which, if I don't get myself paid up with the rental company for what's in the next room, they will damn sure come in here and take everything that's not nailed down. And that includes what you are presently relaxin' on."

"How'd you ever get into such a mess?"

He was beginning to wonder the same about himself.

"Just born poor and managin', so far, to stay like that. Let me tell you something. Aimin' to be a big deal freelance writer is not a helluva' lot different from Oscar's problem. These are lean times for me also. Oscar hasn't got a monopoly on them. Anyway, the bottom line is I've spent everything and then some from what I made on the articles I showed you. And do not ask if my family can help out because they can't. So what you say, Adam? I guess I don't need to tell you that if they take away everything around here, not only are you and I out of business, so to speak, but we are also gonna be doin' our screwin' on the bare floor. Right now, all that's paid up is the rent, but before you know it that'll be comin' due again also."

"Well we can't let this happen."

"Yeah? Whatcha mean by `we', man?  Whatcha mean, `we'?"

"Let me just think a minute. Give me a little time."

"Like Oscar says, we ain't got time to do any of that."

"Shut up. Just shut up. The two of you. Look. I can't just go and write you a check for that kind of money. Clare would have a fit."

"I thought you said payin' me was her idea."

Not too bright to have been carried away and said such a dumb thing.

"Christ, Charlene. What you're askin' for is not what anybody could reasonably consider a payment. It's a downright bail-out."

"Oh just tell her, you know how they put it. Say I've got a temporary cash flow problem. Besides, you guys have plenty of dough."

"All that Clare would hear is the part about there being a problem. And where'd you get the idea we were rolling in dough?"

"Well...the house, the cars, the boat, and you used to be a big deal surgeon. I just figured you for several hundred thou' a year."

"Well figure again because you're dead wrong. We are merely comfortable. That's all. We are not well off and we can stay comfortable only if we're careful."

Meanwhile, from the stereo in the next room, there were sounds of Oscar offering up a musically expressed formula for conduct in circumstances such as these hardly much in keeping with Adam's customary code of behavior. That song also reminded Adam, and sorely so, of Oscar's dim view for his having had anything to do with this woman. How else to take his belting out, to a West Indian tempo, of the proper way to `split' when an affair was finally too hot to handle? Oh to be that casual. For Adam, once committed, tended to be one of those loyal sorts. The price for that was the conversion of a recent tendency towards depression to one bordering on frenzy.

"What you thinkin' about Adam? Look at me, man. You gonna just lay there starin' at the ceiling? What's up? Hell. I didn't figure it to be this much of a drag. You look like a ton of bricks just fell on you. You gonna' cop out on me. Right?"

"No, no. Not at all. There has got to be a way of getting you the money, but we need to do it discretely, so it's just between you and me. Like I said, I can't be writing any checks for that big an amount or Clare is going to hit the ceiling and have all kinds of questions. It could even get back to Oscar and no one can ever figure how that guy's going to react to anything. Look, right now, I've got to get going. While I'm showering I'll kick it around some."

She must have turned up the volume. Even over the shower he could still hear Oscar's voice. Uncanny. So to the point. Now he was singing about some sort of bewilderment in a sexual liaison. Well, that was surely apropos. No way had Adam had any idea of what he might be getting into with this woman.

Then there was another song, probably even more on target, about some kind of an `old fool'. Well, there was nothing like an old fool, for sure. And no doubt about it, either.

Oscar Brown Jr., the astute observer of the human scene had something for everybody. And for all seasons, to boot. But he'd appreciate it, right now, if Oscar would just stifle himself out there. What Adam needed was not any further musical needling from the stereo in the next room but peace and quiet so he could think things out.

Charlene went with him to the door and toyfully restrained him from leaving. Not by force, but with her mouth to his ear and a wriggling finger crooked inside the front of his shirt.

"When you gonna' let me know, honey man?"

"C'mon, Charlene. I gotta' go. There's an answer for everything. I've just gotta' hit on it."

"Yeah, but I've only got a coupla' days before they come and haul everything outa' here. Goodness, Adam. Can it really be you're ready again?"

He pushed her inquiring hand away, not failing to consider that in spite of this sudden hitch, she might still be worth all the pain.

"Haven't you heard? There's supposed to be a connection between pain and pleasure. And it looks like you've managed to set it off."

"So now I'm a pain?"

"Hell no. You're terrific."

"You are going to dump me. Aren't you?"

"Never. I'll be back tomorrow. We'll manage somehow. And try to do some work, will you? When do you suppose we can start getting things down on paper? Clare's even beginning to ask why it is that all we do is talk. Next thing you know we'll also have old Oscar getting antsy for concrete results. We need something to show for the time we're putting in. After all, only a little of it is being spent like this."

He kissed her hard and shoved off.

Driving home he wondered if it was not truly amazing how this conglomeration of atoms of which he was made, and which would soon be blown beyond the limits of his galaxy, maybe even to the far ends of the universe, could possibly have come together so cleverly as to contrive this complicated conspiracy.

Thirteen

Over coffee that same evening, the subject of Charlene was served up once more.

"Well, Adam. How much you planning on?"

"For the new roof? Hell, that's not up to me. Ask the roofer."

"No, dummy. I said planning. Not expecting. How much are you going to pay that woman?"

"How's about five hundred?"

He'd try for at least that amount, legitimately. As for the rest, he still had no idea.

"And that'd be it?"

"Well, I can't be sure. Of course, I'll also have to carry the cost of making copies, revisions, mailings. There's no exact way of knowing. I've never done anything like this before. What I was also thinking, maybe along with the book, trying to package a music video or a CD. Try and give the reader a way to hear or to visualize what Oscar's all about, on the chance of getting them hooked. But that's a whole separate ball game which needs looking into. And maybe we could sell the thing, all over and in clubs or theater lobbies should Oscar get some bookings. There might be more to it beyond what we'll wind up owing Charlene."

Clare was stuck in her groove.

"So right now, we're only being nailed for five hundred? That's it? Right?"

He'd never known her to be so unrelenting. Charlene had become a fixation.

"Far as I can tell."

"Okay. I'll get the checkbook. Do we just mail it?"

"Sure. Why not?"

After all, he wasn't planning to see her for almost eighteen hours.

Clare returned with the checkbook, made one out for his signature, and slipped the signed check into a stamped envelope.

"Where's she live? I'll put it in the morning mail since I'll be headed for the post office anyway. Unless you'd rather drop it off to her."

"No. Your way is more businesslike."

After getting the address from him, she started to write it on the face of envelope, but came to a quick stop.

"Why? But she lives so near us. Doesn't she though? Wouldn't it be just as easy for you to simply go ahead and hand it to her? And maybe Miss Davis would really prefer getting it from you like that, kind of personally."

Adam's heart was skipping about. What was Clare up to? Why couldn't she just lay off on all of this?

"No. I don't want there to be anything personal about it. Let's do it your way. Just mail it."

"Suit yourself; I'm only trying to be helpful. There.

It's all agreed to and done. So what are you planning for tonight?"

"I thought I'd get caught up on our brokerage accounts. Make sure no one is trying to put something over on us. With no earnings coming in anymore, I've got to be damned careful what we do with the pension money and whatever else we have."

"Why don't we just go for treasury notes or municipals and forget all that? Is it really worth the bother?"

"Well we've got to do better than simply keep up with inflation. If you get stuck with long-term treasury notes at six percent when everyone else is earning ten, you're in deep trouble."

"How about gold? Anybody still investing in that? My father used to. And I can remember ten years ago when it was going for almost a thousand dollars an ounce."

Clare, in a blink, had turned providential angel. "Gold? Fantastic. Terrific. I mean... no. Hell. No. No good at all. It doesn't trade anywhere near that anymore."

"Why'd you jump like that? Are you feeling all right? Why on earth would you yell `terrific', then say `no good at all'?"

"I'm okay. Relax. I was just upset my words were getting a little twisted."

"That's a bit hard for me to swallow. You're generally pretty fussy about how you pick them. All right then. So which is it? Is gold a good or a bad investment?"

"Like I said. No good at all."

"Well, that's it. It's all settled. Miss Davis will be getting her money. You'll be watching over ours. And there'll be no gold hoarding in this old house. So if you'll excuse me, I'm going to bed early. Goodnight, Adam."

"Why so early?"

"I'm just a little tired. And no need to go checking my pulse. I'm quite all right. Actually much better now that the chemotherapy is finally finished."

"Goodnight, kiddo."

Bless her. Just like that she'd given him the way out. How could he have forgotten so completely that twelve years before this, when gold really was in favor, he'd bought all those kruggerands? And then stashed them away against a "rainy day." Especially uncanny because one helluva downpour had taken place without his re-membering those darling coins. Here, only as little as six hours ago, and even though he'd been staring up from Charlene's mattress into a veritable torrent of wet stuff pouring by her window, and with her giving him the bad news, and still he'd not been clued to the fact of his rainy day finally having arrived.

Back then, twelve years ago, he'd counted on the coins going up in value. It never happened. Perversely, they'd plummeted. But surely they were still worth a lot of money and all he had to do was retrieve them.

Thank God he could remember where they were. Nowadays, he was starting to forget all sorts of things. The coins must still be where he'd hidden them, for security reasons, in that high corner of his attic.

They'd been emptied into a long and shallow wooden box once containing Camembert cheese, and then he'd cleverly concealed the box up behind an old molding that could be gotten to only by crawling along one of the old overhead beams. Christ! He hoped he was still up to such acrobatics. He'd need to be every bit as agile as he was back then if he was to recover his artfully sequestered coins.

An hour later, sure that Clare was asleep, he headed up into the attic. To climb that beam and get across it was a trial. Not so much because of the contortions required, but because the beam had become filthy dirty over the years. And also because, as it unfortunately turned out, when his roofer had made certain recent repairs for a roof leak, the damned fool had apparently used oversized nails. This meant that their sharp points were protruding into the crawl space above the beam.

Every time that Adam rose up for a breather and to be sure of where he was heading, if he neglected to keep his head down a certain required distance, he was rewarded with very painful reminders of the business ends of those nails and the repair guy's incompetence.

Nevertheless, in about fifteen minutes, he had carried off this entire adventure and was seated on an attic step, Camembert box in hand. Although grimy, and with blood trickling down and across his face from a scalp punctured in multiple places by the nails, it was still a triumphal moment. Fortunately, no rat bent on lingering smells of cheese had scattered them. The kruggerands were all there.

Next, he went back downstairs and out into the garage where he locked his haul inside the trunk of the car. Then, it was into the shower for a third time that day. His problem, or at least the immediate part of securing funds and of doing it secretly, had been solved.

A little antiseptic solution to the scalp, a self-administered shot of tetanus booster just to play it safe, and he could begin to relax. All that remained was to drive down to Deak and Company in the morning and see what they'd give him for the coins.

That night, Adam had a strange dream. He thought, all

night long, he was Jesus Christ. In the morning he decided it was because of all those painful scalp wounds.

To leave the house as he did, well before Clare was up, constituted a unique event for such an ordinarily late riser. But he had to sneak his telltale stigmata past her, without risking any whys or wherefores.

Fourteen

By ten he had parked on K Street and entered the offices of Deak and Company. The cheese box lay concealed in his briefcase.

Adam's feelings were a mix of satisfaction for the apparently successful way his furtive moves were proceeding and apprehension over the increasingly ungovernable complexity of the operations required to pull them off. How could he not be troubled? His basically kind-hearted move in an old friend's interest had so easily escalated into others, rapidly transforming a straightforward kind of person like himself into a deceitful and guilt-ridden sneak?

And all because Oscar and Clare, the profiting or favoring bystanders in this venture of the book, were joined in such vehement opposition to the business of Charlene. If people could just be more flexible and allow others a reasonable latitude of action, there needn't be all of this stressful subterfuge. And he wouldn't be staring, now, into the face of a punctilious clerk looking askance, it seemed, for his right to redeem his hard earned and honestly purchased coins for current fair value.

"May I inquire as to how you came by them, sir?"

"Why do you want to know?"

"Just routine, sir. A mere formality."

"I bought them right here. Around twelve years ago. It could have been your father who sold them to me."

Adam was only trying to strike a light note. But it didn't appear to be working. The clerk's expression remained cool, businesslike. His nametag showed he was a certain Clive Dempsey.

"My father has never been employed by Deak. He's a police detective in Baltimore. Now, sir, what did you say your name was?"

"I didn't, Officer Dempsey."

The need for being surreptitious was really getting him down. So much so, he'd continued mocking the clerk at risk of seeming flippant in order to have himself a little comic relief. Anyway, better flippant than looking suspicious to a fellow from a law and order kind of family, unexpectedly putting him through some sort of a third degree. All Adam had anticipated was a quick, over the counter negotiation and a correspondingly expedited transfer of the proceeds of that altogether simple transaction into Charlene's waiting hands.

"Please sir. It's just Mister Dempsey, if you will. And I'll have to have your name and social security number in order to check our records."

"Grossman. Doctor Adam Grossman. 101421379."

"Oh. You're a doctor? May I ask what kind?"

"I'm a psychiatrist. And I'm going to start taking notes if we can't move this thing along. When someone asks this many questions it always suggests, to my practiced mind, a hint of paranoia."

That little falsehood set Dempsey to moving well enough. He fairly bolted rearwards from his window station towards an array of computers located behind him.

"Back in a moment, sir. Please have a seat over there."

It was more than a moment. It took several minutes for him to return, during which Adam did not particularly take to the idea of having to sit where the clerk had indicated. It was next to an expansive plate glass window and in a wide open public space looking out onto K Street. It was no stretch for him to feel looked at and recognized by each and every passerby. Eventually the fellow was back.

"There we are. It's all in order. Too bad you waited this long to sell. You'd have done a lot better getting out in '82. You'd have made more than double what you're to receive now. But when you stop and consider it, you're still better off than if you'd invested in so many other ways. Sure you don't want to hold onto them? You just might want to stop and think about it. Gold's certain to go up again, sooner or later."

"No. These days I don't have time to stop and think about anything. I'm selling the lot. What are they worth?"

The man tapped away furiously on his countertop keyboard. After awhile he read off a figure, but kind of secretively to himself. Then penning it to a slip of paper, he slid his notation across for Adam's appraisal, at the same time declaring the amount.

"It comes to twelve thousand, four hundred and eighty dollars, and twenty-five cents."

It was a new kind of day. Adam was overjoyed. Turned practically carefree. At least Charlene would not be cleaning him out. He'd figured the coins for less than half of that.

"Good. I'll take it in cash."

"Cash, sir?"

"Cash. That give you some kind of a problem?"

"Well it is very unusual, sir. And also, it's not a very secure way to be going about. This isn't the world's safest city these days. And besides that, may I take you into my confidence?"

"Absolutely. Since your father is a policeman, I have no qualms whatever."

"Well sir, any cash transaction for ten thousand or more has to be reported to the Internal Revenue Service. Know what I mean?"

In truth, Adam hadn't a clue as to where this guy was heading. But all of a sudden he was brought to speculating about all kinds of things... money laundering, tax evasion, even drug deals. One thing he knew for sure, though. This cash arrangement he was entering into with Charlene was absolutely no business of Uncle Sam. He made a quick and shrewd decision.

"I tell you what."

"Yes, sir?"

"Let me have the amount in two equal cashier's checks."

"Why two, sir?"

"I've got two rear pants pockets. That's why."

In another ten minutes Adam was back out on K Street feeding more quarters into his parking meter. Enlightened now by all of this new information about the IRS, his financial machinations of the morning needed to be a little more involved, but it was nothing he couldn't handle.

It took him another half-hour to accomplish his mission.

Immediately close by were branch offices of two banks in which he held accounts. In each he showed his driver's license and cashed one of the checks from Deak and Company.

Emotionally drained, wary of perfectly innocent strangers who might be intending to rob him, but all the same now delightfully cash rich, he headed for Charlene's place.

Fifteen

As he pulled to the curb near her building, his scalp pain, only bothersome before then, became much worse. To examine the affected areas, he rose up to study himself in the rearview mirror and was relieved that there were no conspicuous areas of redness or swelling, just encrusted scabs at places of penetration by the roofing nails.

But his facial appearance was quite another matter. You, he belabored his reflection, are one tormented person. To thinking about it, the Christ dream of the night before was not the least bit farfetched. Did this not feel as it should for the victim of any comparable crucifixion scenario? The head pains, the unavoidable self sacrifice, the cranial stigmata, the whole damn bit?

Sacrifice? Now there was a word for you. And sacrifice for whom? For none other than Oscar Brown Jr. There could be nothing in it for Adam Grossman. So then... why, precisely, had he permitted himself to be bothered to the extent of all this pain and grief?

An answer sprang instantly to mind. It was only because, as was so vehemently trumpeted by the devoted knight's squire in "Man of La Mancha," he liked him, Oscar that is. He really liked him. After all was said and done, Oscar was his friend and he, Adam, really, really liked him. As simple as that.

He pressed the downstairs buzzer.

"Who's there?"

"Santa Claus."

"Come back in December."

"Hey, but I've got all your goodies."

There were instantaneous responses from the door opener, and over the intercom, Charlene.

"Enter, Santa."

The countering line came from a fellow now feeling a little less pain. "It's Christmas in August."

And once upstairs and admitted by her questioned further.

"You've really got it?"

"Check it out."

He gave her one of the envelopes into which he'd crammed five thousand in one-hundred dollar bills. The rest of his haul stayed below, in the car.

"This is wild. You've no idea how relieved I am."

"I'll let you show me."

"Why sure... honey. Go in and make yourself comfortable. I'll be right there."

Two hours on that mattress and Adam had good reason to recant any claim of single-mindedness in Oscar's behalf. Sore scalp and self-sacrificing, self-pitying mood or no, recruitment of this young woman had proved a solid enough venture for time that would have been otherwise wasted.

It had been an oversight to disregard such compelling

evidence that the gloomy doomsday kitchen radio postulation was being pleasurably palliated upon the floor of this apartment. And it would be no stretch to suggest that Charlene had been employed, thus far, mostly as a means for warding off the depressing effects of that revelation.

After all, up to now, for all of their talking and coming together, they'd come up with no reasonable semblance of a literary work product. Nor could it ever be rightfully claimed that Charlene's growing hold on him was in any way to be blamed on Oscar. After all, he'd warned against her.

Charlene was struck by his heightened ardor.

"Hon', I'm afraid you might hurt yourself."

"You mean drop dead?"

"No. It just seems you're getting a little carried away."

"For a guy my age?"

"Oh Adam. Knock it off. It's only that you're all sweated up. And..."

"I know. And it's getting late."

"What's gotten into you, honey? It's not like I'm gonna run away. I'm always here for you. Besides. I have the feeling something's going on in this bed that I don't know about."

"Like what?"

"Can't put my finger on it."

"Oh, c'mon. You have a magic finger. It can do just about anything."

"Don't get smart with me, Adam. This time, when we made love, you were up to something. You were, weren't you?"

"I have no idea what you're talking about. Maybe it

just seemed different because for once we forgot to have Oscar in a sing-along."

"Yeah. All right. Maybe that was it."

This fetching young gal, and as was becoming more and more apparent, this little conniver, had been pretty sharp to pick up on the subtle signs of his secret agenda for countering depression with sexual vigor. But what she couldn't know was that he had started to care about her. Or that his edginess regarding interracial intimacy had completely evaporated.

She remained inquisitive as he readied to leave, but on a different tack.

"How'd you latch onto all that cash, Adam?"

"Can't tell you. It's too embarrassing. Let's just say that where there's a will, there's a way. And if that's not enough for you, remember that in some peoples' book the need justifies the means."

"But that's not you, Adam."

"Already I'm all figured out. Right?"

"Yes. And you can stop playing so damned mysterious. I was probably right in the first place. What you said about your financial situation was pure baloney. Wasn't it? You're loaded. Aren't you? Just holding out on me. Right? Didn't want this little old gal to get her hooks into you too deep. Right? Admit it, Adam. Little Charlene had you figured for a couple hundred thou' a year, minimum, and she was right. And people taking in that kind of dough never have a problem getting their hands on whatever cash they need."

"You are dead wrong."

This was an unanticipated and ugly downturn. His scalp tenderness was back and rapidly changing over into a splitting headache. A personal sort of financial disclosure was not something he'd bargained on. Nor was the unpleasant suspicion of maybe being set up for some kind of exploitation.

"I very much doubt it, honey."

She had closed in on him again, but not for a kiss or to embrace. But to whisper, her lips brushing past an ear, newly made anxious.

"And you just remember my own kind of motto, Mister Doctor Grossman. An honest dollar for an honest day's work. My lawd. You'd think your old money was some kind of handout, or for some kind of services other than our very particular business understanding. Shame on you. I've half a mind to get a lawyer and have him draw up a proper enough contract so's we know exactly where we all are comin' from and headin' for."

She might not be kidding. It was a gnawing enough thought. Even though she'd kissed him soundly enough once more.

"That might not be a bad idea."

"Yeah? Well, while we're about it, why don't we lay it all out plain and simple. Like today? That was my advance. But what about my future runnin' expenses? We gotta deal with them too. I've got overhead, food, rent, incidentals. Long as I'm workin' on this book I can't very well take on other jobs, can I? What we goin' to do about all of that, Doc?"

This was no longer a downturn. A crash was more like it. And best to get the devil out of there without any further commitment.

"We'll have to cross that bridge when..."

"Shit."

"Remember, Charlene. The Lord provides."

"Now look who's the Baptist."

"And He fits very neatly, the back to the burden. Right?"

"We all know about burdens, Adam. Black folks are experts on them. So don't you be one too. Let's just keep the money comin' in as I need it. Okay? After all, it's no more than what's called for. Right, honey? And I'll pass on a written contract. We can just kiss on it. How's that?"

"I'm hearing you."

Their not so solemn understanding was struck as imprecisely and, for him, as misgivingly as that.

Sixteen

That night, he sat before the TV, but stared vacantly at it, brooding. Were he to keep slipping her more and more money, what would he do when it finally ran out?

Estimating what had to be covered for her rent and reasonable expenses, he figured to just about manage another six months. Suppose the book didn't get finished by then? That was a jarring thought. Nor was it particularly agreeable, should they wrap up this writing project in a tidy time frame, that the personal side of their little arrangement, for one or another reason, might go by the board.

None of this anxious speculation, oddly enough, spilled over into any practical concern for the fact that he had yet to see, from this ongoing literary project, as much as a single printed page. All that really concerned him was the shaky nature of their affair, and how to keep her satisfied.

Oscar called at nine-thirty.

"What's happenin'?"

"Why do you always start like that? Why not, straight out, ask me how I am, or how I'm doing, or how Clare might be? And then I could ask you how you were?

Sometimes I get the feeling you are an entirely self-centered person."

"I get it. Nothin's happenin'. That's what. And from the vibrations I'm feelin' you've gone and had your first no-holds-barred brawl with that chick 'a yours. Welcome to the world of little black foxes, Adam. So what's she want for more of the same?"

"You're entirely off base. And everything is proceeding smoothly."

"Yeah, I'll bet. Well out here it's startin' to heat up. L.A. is like a damned tinderbox. All that's needed is some kinda spark to set it off. Like a police incident or the wrong kinda jury verdict."

"Now look here, Oscar. You stay out of it. Please. At least for this year, steer clear of all that stuff."

"Well I may just be able to. Guess what?"

"I'm afraid to ask. What?"

"Looks like Uncle Sam needs me."

"You got yourself drafted at sixty-five?"

"Shit no. I'm bein' considered for some special grant money."

"How's that?"

"The National Endowment for the Arts. They need some people to interact artistically with college kids from Watts."

"Okay. But how's a job like that going to get you anywhere?"

"Well just listen up a minute because it sounds like a real good deal. The grant carries a fair salary and even has some liberal leave time for out-of-town performances. That's if there should be any. Hell. At the very least, it'll pay the rent."

"You'd have to live in Watts?"

"I don't know about that, but I hear this deal also comes with all kinds of perks and chances to meet some big time people."

"It sounds too good to be true."

"Could be. But we'll just wait and see. And you wanna know somethin' else? I'm not so sure anymore, as I've stopped to think about it, that bein' out of the performin' loop has really been such a disaster for me. Man, I'm realizin' more and more that if I'd of been some kinda pop star runnin' every which way and then some, strainin' to do a gig a night, there'd have been no time to write all my hundreds of songs and poems and shows. All in all, when you consider it, it hasn't been the worst thing in the world for me. Because whatever happens, I'm still a success as far as my composin' and my writin' go, even if I'm not makin' the popular scene."

"I see. You've changed your mind about the whole thing. Good deal then. Go and get yourself nationally endowed. No problem at all. We'll just close up shop back here and forget all about the dumb book. Because, as things stand right now, you are guaranteed, no matter what, to be well thought of. At least by yourself and maybe a few other people. So that'll be what we settle for."

"Adam, when you gonna learn to shape up and listen? Didn't I just get through tellin' you how it'll still be cool for me to go out and do shows under this arrangement? And you got anything in particular against me havin' rent money and my kids gettin' to see me full time for a change? None of this has anything at all to do with what you and I are into with the book deal. Besides which, this arrangement lets me tap into all these college kids out here. You know how I just love workin' with them."

"I know all about your lovin', Oscar."

"Quiet. You old dog, you."

"Are you sure you've read all the fine print on this appointment?"

"Hasn't even been formalized yet. But don't you worry none. I plan on negotiatin' whatever's called for."

"All right. Let's talk about something else. You remember how you and I considered taking up your story as if you were dead and that was a double downer? For one, you were gone. And two, you went with hardly anybody really noticing?"

"Uh, huh. How could I forget somethin' like that? But it was you who knocked me off. Mind you, if I went along with it, it wasn't with any fuckin' enthusiasm. And you better know it. Don't get the idea that just because you had me laughin', it was for anythin' but it bein' downright ghoulish. You know, what they call gallows humor. It wouldn't bother me in the least bit if you cut that whole sick thing right out of our book."

"Okay. Because I've had my own second thoughts about it."

"Good. You went and got me resurrected? Hallelujah. I'm feelin' better already. You've breathed new life into me. You can call it *The Resurrection of Oscar*. Get it? Recreation, re-creation? Never mind. Just forget it."

Adam ignored the pun. "Yes. I think that for the sake of dramatic emphasis we were pushing that little snatch of novelty a tad too far."

"A tad? Man, if you don't mind me askin', how much further was there to go? Talk about your big bangs. You had me dead. Cold stone dead. That was one helluva lot more bang than this old nigger would ever want for his buck. And besides, I never thought you were doin' yourself especially proud with your little prematurely dead approach. Only a sick dude of a writer would come up with somethin' like that. I was only goin' along fer the sake 'a harmony. That's all."

"Anyway. The way I see it now is that if people went out and bought a book that read like that, not realizing that your demise was no more than a spoof or a come-on, and if they were to somehow take your passing as the real McCoy, not being clued to you still being very much alive, then..."

"They ain't hardly gonna come a' lookin' for me in performance."

"Exactly. And especially self-defeating would be they're not even wanting to go out and buy your music, if it were still available."

"Yeah. Dead, I'd be a real has been. Wouldn't I though?"

"So let's not be too cute."

"I'll go for that. Besides which, ain't nobody gonna think about signin' no contract with a stiff."

"Agreed to."

"Thank de lawd."

"So we write it as straight biography."

"That's cool with me."

"Which brings us to the next question."

"Move it Adam. There's a nice young lady havin' to pay for this call."

"Where the hell are you?"

"Never you mind that. Just get crackin'."

"You still know anybody at RCA?"

"Not really. Every once and awhile someone rolls a

nickel or two my way as royalties. I never even notice who signs for it. Why you askin?"

"Well. Suppose we approach them and see if they wouldn't be willing to reissue one of your old LPs?"

"Why'd they wanna do that?"

"So we can package a CD along with the book. They'd get increased sales as well as publicity for more sales if the book does well. Like one thing feeding the other. And as I recall, they produced your Broadway show, along with its recording. Anyway, what have they got to lose? Those old records of yours and the show certainly aren't selling anymore. You can't even special order them from the stores. They're strictly collector's items."

"You tryin' to get me down? You want me to start cryin'? One way or another, you mean to do me in, don't you? If you're not killin' me off in print, you're settin' to sell me short."

To see Oscar unemployed and in tears again was the last thing Adam wanted. He remembered once more the lamentable street scene of years before and his haunting memory of Oscar not performing. He'd never want to experience a transition like that again. Nor did he want a reminder of the uneasy closeness of clowning and crying. For Oscar, when he so chose, could be a marvelous clown.

"No way. I'm not putting you down. To the contrary, it seems to me that if we have a recording to package along with the book, people might get a taste for some of your greatest numbers and also sample your voice. But who knows? If RCA would do a deal with us, what the hell, they might get carried away with the idea, go all out, and do a music video and revive the Broadway show."

"I dig it, I dig it. That is one dynamite idea. Look. Soon as this thing is written, let's find out whom we have to talk to and go hit on 'em."

"Nice to hear a little enthusiasm for a change."

"Well, what d'you expect? That's the best damned plan I've heard in years. Got to hand it to you, Adam. When you want, you can be a downright genius. All you have to do is set your mind to it a little more often."

"That's an insult. A genius? You are underestimating me."

Oscar, tucked away in L.A., erupted in deep throated laughter over the nice young lady's telephone.

"Now all we need is for your chick to settle down and into some serious writin'."

"Yes. But on that score we need to get something else clear. There's the matter of Charlene's compensation."

"Yeah. Well I'll leave those little details to you."

For reasons they both understood full well, Oscar chortled his way through that one also.

"Right. Now the deal is that I've given her an out-of-pocket advance. An out-of-my-pocket kind of advance. Get it?"

Adam didn't dare to say how much. Oscar would be screaming bloody murder even if it wasn't his money being spent. To stir him up all over again into venting his suspicions about Charlene was not the way to go.

"I appreciate that. But don't rub it in. Think I like being so underprivileged? Anyway, I hope you didn't go overboard."

Oscar had put it just about right. He believed himself, in every sense, to have gone completely over the side. Hook, line, sinker, the whole bit, over the side. Best to let that bewildering fact, as well as Oscar's admonition, pass uncommented upon.

"The only remaining question is how do we cut her in as we move forward? Conceivably, she'd have legitimate claim to full authorship rights. But since the book is our concept, and she is nowhere without what material we turn over, I think it's more appropriate we divide any earnings or royalties three ways. Any problem with us giving her half and you and me splitting the balance?"

"I sure do. Make it an equal three way split. That's more than generous. And if there's movie rights, then that's just between us. Out of that, the chick draws nothin'. Otherwise we pass. We dump her and we walk."

"Oscar, where we walking to? We've got no damned place to go. Charlene happens to be our writer, our ticket. She is the only game in town."

"Yeah. Thanks to your bein' so pigheaded, she is. Look old buddy, if this is gonna be a biography that is officially authorized by me, then that's how we're gonna play it. Dig? And if this sweet little thing of yours... Remember, you are not foolin' me any, Adam. I know damned well what you two are up to. If she doesn't buy the deal and goes and publishes anything at all without my express consent, I'll do a number on her jus' like the elephant did to the lion. Only I won't be whippin', I'll be suin' her ass and to a fare thee well."

"Look, Mr. Endowed Artist. Don't you think you're having a few too many delusions of grandeur? This whole thing is about getting you off the financial rocks. Remember? And you haven't got the dough for mounting any fancy law suits."

"No sirree. I have no delusions of grandeur. I just have

solid convictions of my own personal worth. Anything about me, like Muhammad Ali used to say, is about `the greatest'. You remember that when you deal with the fox and everything will work out just fine. Gotta go now, Adam. This call's costin' somebody a heap 'a change."

"Hey, Oscar."

"Yeah?"

"Now that we've decided you're not going to die in the book, don't be crapping out on us in the meantime. At least not until Charlene and I have latched onto all your royalties. You know. For the really greatest story ever to be told."

"You are a dirty dog, Adam. Okay, babe. Wait up. I'm comin'."

Seventeen

A dam was dreaming quite a lot these days and the dreams were much the same. Nothing seemed to work. Everything fell short of expectations.

The last one was in keeping with all the others. Vaguely out there, somewhere, was Clare, who appeared to have been abandoned and needed him. Was it at some roadside place where he'd hoped to pick her up? But then there were other demanding persons with whom he had agreed to meet up with.

One of them was a certain young doctor who lived across the way on an island. But Adam lived on a different island with limited flight schedules to that of the young doctor. So how on earth was he to pack up and transport himself there in the required short space of one hour, if there was not a single flight to be had in less than five?

For some reason, logic dictated the solution of driving to this other island, but in his aging car which unfortunately proceeded to stall out as it passed across a sagging and unstable bridge span. By deserting his car and resorting to an elevator-assisted descent, cleverly conceived though it was, he gained himself nothing, getting as usual, nowhere at all.

In real life, also, was he not just stumbling this way or that, frustrated by a similarly purposeless and queer kind of existence? Perhaps this was destined for a man reaching his age, particularly if he stops working and no longer has the daily tasks that were routine for half a lifetime. Or was this what happens nearer to life's end? Rather than fewer, there are more than the usual number of unpredictable demands and distractions to be coped with.

It was hard, though, for him to lay the blame on life's seeming ingenuity for dealing out devilish vicissitudes when all of his complex and tedious involvements were entirely of his own making. Not the least of which was Adam's all consuming fixation on self-indulgence with Charlene, his frantic device for avoiding glum thoughts of a starry extinction.

But how could eroticism, entered into by dint of desperation, be looked to for any kind of satisfactory sustenance? It was certainly not turning out that way with Charlene. Which even led him to wonder if it would not be better, after all was said and done, to simply settle for a generous earful of Bach, all the way to Armageddon.

But Charlene had her hold on him. So much so that he tended to forget what she was supposed to be engaged at. The book had become secondary, no more than an excuse for having her. The rub was that Adam had not only *this* obsession but also his friend, Oscar, a long held fascination. And of course, there was Clare, his devotion.

Such were his swirling concerns as he lay in bed the

following morning, awaiting as usual, Clare's customary and dedicated effort to mobilize him. It was not long in coming.

"You all right, Adam?"

"No. I'm like everyone else. Waiting for the end."

Adam had chosen not to make Clare privy to his mind-bending late night broadcast. He knew that unlike himself, she'd not have been the least bit fazed, because of her levelheaded practical mindedness. Or that failing her, then a certain religious bent would not be likely to let her down.

"Well good. I see you're feeling lots better. So rise and shine."

"Now you're some kind of a drill sergeant?"

"C'mon, get up. It doesn't do you any good lying there. Why can't you ever be like most people? They try to be practical. They take situations as they come and just keep moving on."

"Well, I'm me. I'm not other people. And these days being up and about doesn't seem to get me anywhere. All I manage is more chores, more headaches. So why bother getting up at all? Why not just stay right here in bed and out of trouble?"

"Was I not led to understand you were palming off the only really chore you had? Onto that person? What's her name again?"

"Charlene, Charlene Davis. Only the writing part. I'm still the one responsible for choosing everything that goes into it. Step by step, I have to come up with the overall conception. She's no more than a mere technical resource."

"I'll bet."

"What's that supposed to mean?"

"Now don't start getting mad, Adam. But you are a changed person. And it's surely not from going back and forth to the hospital and hanging out with some of your old cronies. I just want you to know that whatever you're up to, it's all right with me if it would only make you happy. But anyone can see you're not. So why don't you just pick yourself up and do something different? Why not hop out to California and hang out with Oscar for awhile? Or take off in your boat? You could go for a nice long cruise up and down the bay. You could even see about getting back into practice with someone. All this introspection and mucking about is not good for you."

"The book, Clare. Remember the book?"

"I take it all back. Forget about the book. You've got to start thinking about yourself if going on like this means having you so miserable."

"Well maybe in a while I will do something different. But right now, Oscar, you, me, we three have all agreed that old Adam's got himself a heavy commitment."

"Not if it means killing yourself over it."

"For me that's exactly what it means. To the bloody death, babe. If that's what it calls for. Something like our own commitment. No?"

"Well then, get yourself out of bed and move on with it. If you have to go berserk or knock yourself off, better do it while I'm still around, either to pick up or to bury the pieces."

"Talk about being morbid. But you know, you're carrying on so about doing something different reminds me of a call I got the other day. I might just take a stab at it. This big shot lawyer I know asked if I would review a malpractice case from the standpoint of testifying."

"Forget it, Adam. That stands to be nothing but trouble. What are you thinking? How could you ever consider, at this late stage of your career, something like that? What are you? An absolute glutton for punishment? You start testifying and that's the end of your good name. It's also the end, should you ever decide on it, of any chance for getting back into practice."

"Yes. But it sounds like such an open and shut case. The only reason this patient died was that a chest tube was improperly placed. And guess who the surgeon was. None other than the little bastard who made life miserable for yours truly. I tell you, going into court on this one would be the kind of doing good that I could feel just great about. Christ. But I'd like to take it on."

"I'm going back downstairs. I can't take any more of this. You've got me living in a nut house. For all I care you can stay in bed forever. Want me to bring you up some breakfast?"

"No, no. I'll be down."

The more he thought about it, Clare was probably right. But for a different reason. Why add involvement in a messy malpractice suit to his other tumult, the affair with Charlene?

And yet, he was tempted to do it. The idea of making public declaration of this man's incompetence and of seeing him suffer the humiliation of an adverse jury verdict, was truly inviting.

The only other way of getting back at the guy was pure fantasy. He'd catch up with him some dark night and maybe beat the hell out of him. Or worse? Why sure. In some other time, or even this one, a really put-out fellow might not have much hesitation in doing something like that. An interesting twist, was it not? Talk about taking one's pleasure from that which stood to be defunct.

A really put-out fellow? Like a demented one perhaps? As if to agree he'd become at least a little crazy? And Clare was right? That he had, in fact, converted their home into a "nut house"? Who, after all but a "nut", could feel like Jesus Christ one minute, and then be having thoughts that alternated between taking an old man's pleasure with a young woman and planning murderous kinds of revenge upon an offensive colleague?

He put aside his speculations. Besides, he was not a nut. He was perfectly normal. Adam was long convinced that men, and women as well, for all their covering up under tidy clothes and artificial odors, were still much like they'd started out, brutes of heart and mind.

But oh. So much better to be like Oscar Brown Jr. If only he, Adam, just once in awhile, could with words and music, gesture and movement, set aside, as Oscar did, all fearful tribulations. And not give so much as a damn for whether or not he left behind some sort of eternal trail.

Eighteen

This time, he arrived a few minutes early. There was a delay before she let him in and the experience of a distinctly different odor.

"You been cooking?"

"No. Why?"

"It smells different in here."

"Who are you? The local scent hound?"

"Maybe it's just a little musty. It could be the weather."

"Should I open a window?"

"Not on my account. Look. It's no big deal. I just thought it smelled different. Like I said, kind of musty."

"Hey. I think I know what you're talking about. Because I'm smelling it too and I remember. There was someone here, about an hour ago."

She seemed so peculiarly proud to be imparting her little confidence. Or was it relief to have hit upon a suitable alibi for some kind of mysterious guest? Anyway, the mystery was dissolved in short order.

"It was my landlord. And I tell you, Adam, he is just about as seedy as they come, and so persistent. That's who you're smellin'. I'd have told you anyway. Because now there's another little difficulty, honey."

"Charlene, you've got the rent money and then some. What kind of difficulty?"

"Well like you see, when I got here eight months ago, I sort of took over what was left of my girl friend's lease on this here apartment. She went home to Ohio and I took the place over on a month to month basis for the time that wasn't expired. What I didn't know was that when the lease was finally up last month, she had her security deposit mailed back to her. And now the landlord's wantin' me to sign a new lease and come up with a security deposit of my own."

"What's it gonna come to this time, Charlene?"

"Two thou'."

"My God. Two thousand dollars?"

"He won't take pesos, Adam. If that's what you're thinkin'."

"What the devil is he securing? Your furniture is all rented out and it isn't set to explode, is it? So what's he afraid of? That you'll take off with his bath tub? The stove?"

"Listen. 'Round here, Adam, and even in some fancy places I know of, that could just about happen. There are people who move into nice places like this, tear out everything and take off with it. It may be all very strange to you, but I know exactly where this landlord guy's comin' from. Believe me. I've been there."

"When's it come due?"

"End of the week. Gee, Adam. I'm sorry, but how was I to know this was gonna' happen? It took me by surprise, too. Come on now, let's forget it for awhile and see if we can't get you feelin' comfortable."

An hour later, while staring up at the ceiling from his privileged position on her mattress, he worked his way, in secret, through some crucial calculations. From a purely literary standpoint, and that's the only angle he should really be considering, this undertaking, now of seven weeks duration, was a total bust. And for those other services thus far rendered, it would indeed be a very well heeled gent able to pick up the kind of tab he was bearing. By just quick estimate, and throwing in this extra two thousand, it would easily come to, at bare minimum, three hundred dollars a session (or whatever else it could be called) at Charlene's apartment. Not that he wasn't ever the more taken with her each time he left the place, but somehow this entire business had to be gotten on track and become a business project and a productive one, at that.

"Okay. Time's up with me... too."

"What in hell you talkin' about?"

"You've shown me you can write. And this whole deal rests on it. So let's get a move on. There can't be any more time for wasting. Don't look now, but I am also knocking on your door, Charlene. From here on in, make like I'm just another one of those bill collectors outside your door and demanding full payment. And I don't mind saying or else, either. Now this is the first time I've put it to you this way but I've no choice in the matter except to hang tough. You have simply got to start writing. You cannot stall any longer."

"You call this wastin' time, Adam? Now you've really hurt my feelings."

"We are not talking about this kind of time, Charlene. We are talking about the other twenty-one hours still remaining in most days."

"Hey. You think it's so easy, the minute you tear out of here, for me to just settle down and start bein' creative? I'm not a machine, mister. I've got feelings, you know. Especially since I do believe you're startin' to act like maybe you care a little. You don't think I'm any less involved, do you? 'Cause if you do, then I think that's real lousy."

"Look. If to get you started, it means I have to give you a breather, I'm all for it. Finally Charlene, we have to put first things first. We have got to bite the bullet and get down to our original first order of business. Oscar, Clare, and me, the three of us, we stand to be on your back about it."

All of this had been addressed to the ceiling. Adam turned onto one elbow and looked into Charlene's soft young eyes, then at her beguiling mouth. After a moment, she began to nod in accommodation to his insistence that in the interest of finally writing something, there'd be a respite. As she did so, his gaze lowered and he found himself staring at her delicate throat.

"Okay, you go on out of here and let me get to work. But you'll at least come back tomorrow with the other two thou', won't you?"

Was he suddenly on to the one track this girl's mind really stayed glued to?

"Right."

Adam continued to stare at Charlene's throat. He was fascinated by his inclination to take it in both hands and ever so gently, but still firmly and determinedly, wring it. He knew for certain, and it was quite disconcerting to him, that doing so would probably make him feel a hell of lot better.

Once outside, Adam elected to walk for awhile through

the Adams Morgan district. Right now, he needed to stay on the move. Just to sit somewhere thinking about his reshaped arrangement with Charlene, would not be good. He was too pent up and needed distraction, anything to ease his edginess. He thought the best way to bring that about was to walk around briskly in this unfamiliar place among different kinds of people. Adams Morgan reminded him somewhat of New York's Greenwich Village. In recent years it had become increasingly Hispanic but it was also a bustling little enclave crowded with Italian restaurants and artsy little shops catering to shoppers of diverse racial mix.

Why this anger he wondered? Why these temptations to become outright violent? Was he so hooked on Charlene that her all-too-easy readiness to put sex on hold could enrage him that much, although it was his idea, not hers? Or, was he being inflamed, rather, by a growing suspicion she was manipulating, or worse, using him? But earlier on this very day, he had had that same much too quick thought of doing violence. He had almost reflexively fancied an agreeable disposal of the new chief of his department. Had that readiness for mayhem lingered only to unhinge him, tainting his mood and turning him against Charlene with only scant provocation? Or had his life just suddenly become an all too complicated unmanageable mess, what with cataclysms galore, Oscar, Clare, the damned book, unpredictable Charlene, and stashed away kruggerands? How could one ever expect to come up with credible answers to questions like these?

Adam was suddenly diverted from his brooding.

"Hey man. You buyin' today?"

"What are you selling?"

To Adam, that seemed a reasonable enough response

to only a vaguely put offering. After all, the young, well-dressed black man was just standing there in the doorway of an empty shop, hands in pocket, with nothing obvious for sale and there was no nearby push cart or display table. He chanced to recall how as a kid on a New York street, he had been approached in much the same way. But those guys usually carried paper bags or cardboard boxes crammed full of stolen goods, often sweaters or other kinds of clothing.

"You some kind of smart assed dude. Whatcha want? A demo? Shit, old man, make a buy or split. Move it. I don't need to be no street attraction."

"Sorry."

"Man. Don't just stand there apologizin'. Buy or bye. Dig?"

By Adam's dawning stare, each of them realized, just about the same time, there had been a serious mistake and they struck out hastily in opposite directions. But in the man's turbulent wake there trailed a rather sweet and musty odor. Was it from his breath, Adam wondered, or had the fellow's clothing simply reeked of it? If it did, this was not a very discrete drug dealer. Anyway, how could he be? He was much too brazenly outspoken. Yet things might very well be getting like that, not only here, but in other neighborhoods of this "murder capital of the world." Having thought the matter through, Adam was ready to forego further astuteness regarding the Washington drug scene and let the whole incident pass.

But that smell. He knew that smell. Not as strong but definitely just as sweet, and how had he called it for her? "Musty?" Yes, musty. Musty it certainly was. And also it was the smell of marijuana. Marijuana it most definitely was. No missing that smell now. How could he possibly not have recognized it back at Charlene's apartment? He himself had smoked marijuana a few times, many years ago, back in the sixties. Who hadn't? It was everywhere. Oscar too, always had it with him. That's how people partied in those days. He had never taken to it. Pot made him altogether too relaxed and sleepy. Besides, even then, he was already very much the emerging control person and not inclined to hang loose about anything. Nowadays, it was alcohol that was in, but only in modest amounts. Enough to relax, to get a little high, and to elevate the high density lipoproteins in the blood so as to ward off heart attacks, but not so much as to make it dangerous to operate a car.

Christ. Why was his dumb brain raving on like this over every kind of nonsensical irrelevancy when the only fit subject for it to zero in on was that his sexy little Charlene was standing to be a god damned liar. Was that where his money was really going? For marijuana? Talk about tribulations. Now he really had cause for self-torment.

Or was he dead wrong? Maybe it actually was the landlord who caused that lush odor in her apartment. Or had Adam's nose just been playing tricks on him? Or, was it not Charlene, or the landlord, but still some other person who had imparted that musty, that sweet musty, now well remembered fragrance into her place?

Without having any idea of his intent, Adam, careening away from his all too insightful doorway encounter with the underworld of Adams Morgan, made for a quick return to Sixteenth Street and Columbia Road. Soon, breathing heavily, he could see his car in the distance. In another few rapidly taken steps he could also make out clearly, a man and woman talking to one another at the entrance to her building. Their exchange looked somewhat furtive. He could not recognize the man but the woman was Charlene. Just as Adam raised his arm and prepared to call out to her, she pressed something into the strange man's hand and bolted back into the building. The man walked away with a sort of casual, innocent swagger that belied the very contrary nature of what he had been up to with Charlene.

Adam had choices. He could storm back to Charlene's apartment and insist on knowing who in hell the stranger was. And as long as he was asking questions, he could also bring up the subject of the marijuana and whatever else required explanation. Or, he could get in his car, drive away, and rather than involve himself any further in uncertainties and the improbability of getting better than unverifiable answers from Charlene, just beat it back home and count his residual blessings and assets. After all, they were considerable enough to be consoling.

Wasn't that what he truly needed? Healing consolation for a pride wounded by his bad error of judgment in trusting this woman? How, conceivably, at least right now, could he turn to Charlene for anything? Unless he was prepared to buy into whatever she might offer up as dissuasion. Obviously, that could not be.

And there was also the distinct chance Charlene might turn on him in female fury and it wouldn't make the slightest difference whether her rage was genuine or feigned. The result would be the same. No book and no more sexual encounters. So challenge her for what? The merely cathartic satisfaction of venting his indignation. He didn't and couldn't possibly get to know exactly what sort of shady thing was going on. And if a little lying over a marijuana habit was the full extent of it and there was no hidden, larger conspiracy at play against him, hey, why not give the luscious girl a break?

Adam got in his car and headed home.

No doubt about it, he decided. His immediate reactions had been bestial. Knowing them or not for their true nature it remained hard for him to temper his feelings. Other men, no more disbelieving or slighted than he, could really strangle a girl like this, either on suspicion of her lying, or being manipulative, or for just seeming to suggest a sexual kind of rebuff. He had been startled to sense in himself some of that same kind of warp. Fortunately, he was not put together quite that way.

But now a single question pressed for answering. Would not bestial, even if violent, be the better behavior? Primitive feelings and actions subverted contemplation. They annulled thoughtful susceptibility to a troubling and dreadful reality. And for Adam reality had become the horrid, mindless, meaningless, slow ticking through time of indifferent self-destructive orbs arrogant humans called their universe. A universe predetermined every once in awhile to sort itself out into varied configurations, irrelevant to anything, and far from having any concerns whatever for man, only one of its mere tag along rearrangements. Man, no more than a single, transient, apprehensively fidgety, chance form of fate's particulate embodiment. As things were going, if to exist as his kind of ruminating but suffering life form was some kind of a miracle, it was a pretty worthless one at that. Would it not be better to just boil over, know no more than resentful rage, and bust things up a bit?

Nineteen

That evening, Adam listened to a 1966 recording of Oscar in performance at a Cleveland theater. There was a fast moving tempo set to the drum beat and maniacal chanting of Pierre Petain, who had started out in life as a jabbering Haitian with scat and voodoo leanings. There was also the smooth and sensual voice of Lana Carson along with Carlos Hernandez hovering his catchy, rhythmic, guitar in a nasal, confidentially persuasive voice. Another fellow whose name he could not recall was on accordion. And of course, through it all, Oscar. Oscar the composer, but also Oscar the unique, fun loving, finger pointing dynamo of line, music, and movement.

Clare came in to listen.

"It's just marvelous. Isn't it? Don't you worry you may wear out that tape?"

"I take no chances. It's only a copy. The reel-to-reel original, a reel-to-reel copy, and second-generation cassette copies are all carefully set aside."

"Goodness, they'll last forever."

"You really want to discuss that possibility?"

"Make believe I didn't say anything, Adam."

"Well anyway, depending on the type and the quality, most tapes eventually undergo print-through and other kinds of deterioration. They can even be attacked by fungus."

"Who would have thought? I just took it for granted..."

"Yeah, I know. Forever."

"Adam, you don't have to be so antagonizing."

"For Christ sake, Clare. Just sit down and get with the music. That's why I'm playing it. For a better mood. To be like those people were back in '66 when they were doing it. Not that they stayed upbeat when they went off stage. I know enough of what was bugging each one of them to know better. They had their everyday problems, just like anyone else, you name it, every kind of drag. But for them, at least when they were up there on that stage, and for us in the audience, they made it like somewhere else. Hell. It was an out-of-body experience and being out of our crumby kind of world, also. However they carried it off, with the chest thumping beat, with music, the girls' legs, the booze, and God knows what else... it was the best damned way to be. It was life on a lower, not a highest level, but you know what? To get hooked on something like that and forgetting of the real world, this damned unforgiving and heartless place, may be the best thing a person can do."

"Shut it off, Adam. Shut it off. I want to know right now what's biting you. Come on. Shut it off."

She was really charged up. Adam knew he had allowed himself to get a little carried away. Starting with no more than venturesome remembrance, he had shifted into what sounded like a tirade. No point to having Clare overly upset and even more suspicious. What was needed now was some comic relief. He made with a wink and an Oscar kind of comment.

"But, I was cool."

"Cool? You call that being cool?"

"Come on. Don't make a federal case out of it. I was only thinking out loud. You know, in line with seeing more to our book than it being just a pitch in Oscar's interest."

"That life's too dreary and that Oscar could provide an escape? Help us forget? You're trying to tell me that?"

"Right. That's all. From the beginning, I've only seen this business as a way of promoting Oscar so he can make a better living. I haven't given thought at all to what Oscar actually can do for people. He can mean a lot. So the real tragedy may be more in line with what the public is being deprived of than how Oscar is losing out by not receiving, on the face of his merits, what's due him."

"You are not fooling me one bit. That is just jive. Something is bugging you and I know it. You started out by suggesting you just had to play this stuff right now. Right now. Remember? You needed to play it to get some kind of a lift. I want to know what's got you so damned down. God knows, you've been depressed enough lately, anyway. So please, Adam, what is it that's made you worse and straining so for a way out? Coming up with better reasons to write the book is all very nice, but why are you carrying on and having all of this big sudden need to lose yourself in Oscar's kind of music?"

Adam could hardly tell Clare his agonizing truth. There wasn't any chance he could outrightly say, "Well, I'm having an affair with Charlene. Believe it or not, your presumably faithful, sixty-six-year-old husband is totally hooked on having intercourse two, sometimes three times a day, with a thirty-year old gal. But that part of it is A-okay. Problem is I'm paying through the nose for it. And I'm doing it on the sly with our precious kruggerands which I stashed away against a rainy day. Even worse, Charlene, whom I've grown to care for, may not be a truthful person, might even be a drug user, and has yet to type a single page."

Maybe there were fellows out there who could be that brutally forthcoming with an adoring wife of more than forty years living with the fearful problem of ovarian cancer in an uncertain stage of remission. He wasn't one of them. Could be, there were also guys who'd flare up excitedly and say something like that even if they had no good reason to believe they were into anything more than a mid-life, much less an end of the life, fling. He wasn't one of them, either. Adam was simply your average, everyday, considerate kind of a liar.

"You've got it all wrong. You're making too much of absolutely nothing. I'd just rather listen to Oscar than drink scotch. That's all."

"You sure, Adam? Or do I really have to start worrying about you?"

"Go to bed, Clare. I'm okay. I'll be coming up soon as I put these tapes away."

Twenty

Now, Adam would hardly sleep at all. And through that particular night Clare lay vigilant. Each time he stirred, or when he rose for the bathroom, it was "You all right?"

He took breakfast again early, anxious to see how Charlene looked, now that she was under suspicion. But his problematic young collaborator acted and appeared much the same. She was the one, however, to introduce the subject of his concern.

"Hey, where'd you go once you left here yesterday?"

"Why do you ask?"

"Nothing. Only I saw your car was still there an hour later. I went downstairs to pay a guy for running some errands for me."

What was she up to? Covering up? Had she seen him coming along in the distance as well as his parked car? So many, too many, doubts and questions.

"I just went for a walk. Some of the new shops around here are interesting. Anyway, here's the money."

Uncanny. He inclined to reward her but hated himself for it.

"Well. All right then. That should just about do it. Thank goodness, I'm completely bailed out. Don't know how to thank you, Adam. Especially as how we've got our new little understandin' and we're on a serious work schedule. That's still it, right?"

"Correct, girl. I simply have to hold off if that's what it's going to take. Don't get any idea, though, I'm not thinking about you full time. Because I certainly am."

"Hey. Adam honey? I hate to see you looking so down. I'm wondering if this is the best thing for either one of us."

"It may or may not be. The more important question is are you going to finally get yourself settled in and writing?"

Charlene rose up on her toes and delivered the slightest possible non-provocative peck upon his forehead.

"Come back here in three days, Adam, and you will have yourself at least the first thirty pages, maybe more. I'm determined to show you what I can do. Once I get going on something, why, I'm a damned work horse."

"See you then, girl. I'll be looking forward to it."

Adam did not tarry this time. He drove away. He had no taste for seeing any more shadowy people or questionable transactions. His relationship with Charlene would be on hold. There wouldn't even be his customary phone calls. She was well enough fixed for money. She had the recordings and other material. He'd not disturb her in any way. It was now or never.

Another thing. He had to fancy himself less of the liar he actually was. All of that business about being at the hospital every day for get-togethers, coffee and sandwiches.

It was time to impart at least some truth to that spiel, even if it was done now, long past the alleged happenings. Unfathomably, it would make him feel better.

So he drove across town and parked behind his old hospital, entered a back door to the doctors' lounge, poured himself a cup of coffee, and sat down, as he had formerly through many years, to read the morning paper.

"Adam, you old dog."

It was Bilar, chief of Infectious Disease.

"Hey there, how's it going?"

"Same old grind. Not lucky like you. I can't get out that easily. Not that they wouldn't like to push me into early retirement, also. The Dean is forever jabbering, not even just insinuating anymore, about how he'd like to take on a much younger man. And someone who writes an article almost as regularly as he goes to the john. But I just ignore him. I know he's afraid I'll charge him with age discrimination, the son of a bitch. Besides, I've got tenure and there's no way to dump me until I'm damned good and ready to go. And there's no chance, either, they'd offer me the kind of golden parachute you got. They hate me too, but not like they hated you."

"Thanks a lot. I'm sure you meant that kindly."

"Why sure. Hell, you were the only standup guy we had around here. Everyone else just watches his tail. Nobody criticizes anybody for anything anymore. The result is it's disgusting how some of these new guys think they can carry on. You know, the young turks. Feel they can get away with just about anything. And they act like we're lucky to have them on board. But you know, I have never seen so many infections as we're getting now, particularly from the operating room. Hell. Half the time these young geniuses don't even bother to cover their damned noses when they operate. Have some cockeyed idea, I suppose, their dirty schnozzles are sterile."

"Really? What's the post-op infection rate running these days?"

"Runs around seven percent, right now. That's about three times what it used to be. And you know what? The worst damned offender was that new chief of your department. He must have been a real slob. Before he stopped, his was fourteen percent."

Adam thought he felt his heart pound or flutter.

"What do you mean, stopped?"

"Kaput man, kaput."

"A coronary? He's dead?"

Bilar shook his head, "Nobody told you?"

"Told me what? What's to tell? Come on Bilar. You're the first one I've talked to in months."

"He's HIV positive. He's got AIDS."

"You're kidding."

"Who in hell would kid about something like that? I ran the confirmatory in my own lab."

It was stupendous. Not that the nasty young fellow had gotten himself infected with a deadly virus. No, what was astonishing was how quickly Adam was somewhat relieved by that piece of news. And it wasn't that he exulted in the other man's misfortune because he hated him. This day, there was absolutely none of that kind of mean spiritedness. It was purely and simply that he would no longer be plagued by having to fantasize ways of getting back at the bugger, of somehow personally doing him in. It had all been arranged for, without any bother on his part.

"How'd it happen?"

"No one really knows for certain. But he did operate on a few patients who were HIV positive. And what they say is he was always tearing his surgical gloves on something or other during thoracotomies. But you know how it is. All you need is a little skin puncture with the wrong patient and that's it. You've bought it."

"Is he still around?"

"Nope. Took a leave of absence. They made it compensable for him."

"Who's running the department?"

"Can't tell you that either. One of the other men is probably acting chief until they form a search committee for a new head. You want to come back?"

"Can't. My retirement contract won't permit it. How come you're asking? You know damned well, according to the bylaws, department heads have to step down at sixty-five unless the executive committee pushes through some kind of special exception."

"Didn't mean as chief. I heard you pulled out because he was making it rough for you. Now, you could just be a ranking member of the department."

"No. I'm gone for good. My yeoman's days are over and done with and my retirement deal is only as sweet as it is because I agreed to sever and to stay severed."

"So what you doing here today?"

Again, wouldn't it be easy, though, if you could just mouth the truth? Easy, sure. But then, how do you go about explaining it? How to possibly get old Bilar to understand that Adam was sitting there in the doctors' lounge because on previous days that's where Clare understood him to be when actually he was rolling around on Charlene's mattress? And that now he was just doing his best to make good on that prior misrepresentation, in a totally inappropriate and illogical way, by being there at present, long after the fact of his having been quite elsewhere. Of course, it could come about that this same Bilar, at some time in the future, no longer remembering precisely when he'd run across Adam at the hospital, might under the very unlikely requirement of being asked, mistakenly vouch for Adam's presence at the earlier time.

"Today? Oh, I drop by once in awhile in case there's some mail for me."

"Take care of yourself, Adam."

Bilar turned to leave.

"You too, Bilar."

Adam's heavy mood had lifted a little bit. It was better not to feel the strain of his old resentment and vengeful-ness. The new chief had had him going like that for more than a year. And now, the guy was practically dead and gone. But still, there was no actual joy in it. He had no positive feelings. In fact, he still had no idea of how to have that happen anymore. Fate had deflated him. Ev-eryone else might manage a good time, especially Oscar and those who liked to watch him perform. But the only pleasure Adam could manage was Charlene. At least for the time being, that was off. So, pathetically enough, all there was for him was this small, half-hearted lifting of a burdensome poisonous grudge.

He finished his coffee and his newspaper, checked the mail, and left for home.

Twenty-one

Coming through the door, Adam was greeted by the wolfhound, panting, pawing at him, and appearing excited. Next came the Doberman, but just as quickly she was gone again, scampering back toward the living room, as if to declare something important. Clare could be heard there, in conversation. Entering, he saw she was with Oscar.

"Adam."

"They fired you already?"

"No, no. Actually signed a contract yesterday. Just passing through real quick and stopping by for a few minutes. I had a call to do another benefit here in Washington and also a gig in Baltimore. Got to be back on the job in California in two days. Good to see you, Adam. But you know, I agree with Clare."

"How's that?"

"You look real tired."

"Yeah, well. We also serve who do all the work. I'd much prefer to be like you, a jet-setting bon vivant."

"Is that what you call ridin' the red eye between here and L.A.?"

"Why sure, man. I can just see you up there cacklin' and cavortin' along at twenty thousand feet with everybody asking, who is that funny fellow? While down here it's all so much, how do you call it?"

"Slavin,' man. Slavin'."

"Correct. Well, what's all happening in the extended spirit world of Robeson, Bojangles, Martin Luther King and let's not forget that dear old boy Malcolm X?"

"Adam, why you in such a piss poor mood?"

Clare rose from her chair.

"Hey guys, I see this is going to be one of those. I'm heading for the kitchen. It's nice and peaceful there. Would you like something, Oscar? Maybe a hamburger?"

"That'd be just fine. Thanks Clare."

She left and they eyed one another. Adam was not quite sure why he had been picking on Oscar. In fact, he was already remorseful.

"Sorry, Oscar. I guess I'm jealous."

"Of what? You doin' all right."

"I suppose I am. I even have a little something to celebrate. The bastard who was making my life miserable before I quit is having his own troubles now and in fact, they're going to be fatal."

"Adam, I do not waste my time dwellin' on thoughts like that. Gettin' all riled up over some mother fucker out to do me dirt doesn't promote anything. It's better to just walk away."

"Accentuate the positive, eliminate the negative, right?"

"Now you've got it."

"Problem is, I can't. Last night I was playing one of your tapes. Clare was listening also. It reminded me of how I managed to really have fun back in the sixties. That's all beyond me now. And listening to that old recording is nothing compared to what it was like, actually being there. Even then, though, for me it was just the high of one or two nights. I suppose that what I envy you most for is that you can pull off something like that whenever and wherever. You could do it now, right here, in this room. I know you have your aches and pains like anyone else and you're not in a position to put on shows or draw crowds. But you've got it where it counts, up there in your head. Something to get you by the downside of things right up to when you're finally done with all of this nonsense. I was telling Clare only last night, that to give people even the smallest taste of what you do may, after all, be the best possible way to spend my time nowadays."

"I appreciate what you're sayin'. But there's somethin' we got to get straight on, Adam. It's that I have no damned regrets about anything. If I had it to do all over again, chances are I'd do things just the same. Sure, I could have made a helluva lot'a money by cavin'. By just bein' upbeat and not insistin' on my integrity. By not singin' the truth about life as black people feel it. And that's right, by not movin' on in step with all those great departed people you were just bein' so snippy about, including Robeson, Martin, Douglas, Malcolm. Hell. There are hundreds of others I could name. But cavin' is not something I can do. As much as I want to have my music and my songs pay off, I'm not about to do anything like that. And I'm remindin' you again there's no documented reason why I never clicked commercially. Just like for when my New York show folded, I only have my suspicions. That's all. There isn't proof of anything. I just know that when songs that have been among my biggest hits to this very day always managed anyway to rile things up in management circles, then there's a pretty good clue right there as to what was actually goin' on. To them I was an uppity nigger. Of course, in New York it was quite another thing. There was that god damned tax advantage for those investors needin' to be nailed down and it also wasn't too cool stormin' around singin' "don't look now but it's all over for you, whitey."

"But you still think that a book about all this is a good idea, don't you?"

"Maybe. Let's just see how it turns out. But be clear on what I'm sayin'. I've got to be true to what I believe in. And my material, if people really listen to it and give it a chance, sells itself. Like this far out musician was tellin' me only yesterday, 'Oscar, you don't have anything but hits.' Adam, all my songs could be hits. That's if they got to be recorded and performed, they could."

"And if they're taken as intended, right?"

"Intended? Look, I'll say it loud and clear: black people, includin' me and most other black artists, we are presentin' ourselves with the same good intentions and in the same spirit people have always responded to. We are only sayin' the same thing that Shakespeare said, and yes, that Jesus Christ said. We are on the side that is against evil. And fuck any mother fuckers who are for evil."

"Boy, oh boy, you are on a roll now."

"Not really. I just keep workin' at it any time and every time. All I care about is doin' my level best, in my spirit and in the spirit of black people. And not only in the spirit of those famous black persons we are always namin', but also of ordinary black folk who, considerin' what they manage to accomplish, in spite of what they have to put up with, may be doin' the most of all. And tonight, that is exactly what I will do. I will put on the best damned performance I possibly can. That's if I last that long."

"You feeling sick?"

"No, just rememberin' how you're all hung up on this dyin' thing, this end of the universe trip of yours."

"It gets you going, hey?"

"It does like hell. I'm not equipped for dealin' with anything but the present. Who cares what someone may think of me a million years from now? The present is the only thing I know, that I'm constructed to deal with. And Adam, wouldn't you feel damned foolish if you go and die and then, right afterward, someone comes up with a new theory? That there never was a big bang in the first place, so how can there ever be another one? And you went and moped around in the precious little time you had, over just about nothin'? Ever stop and think that even if your explosion is really comin', before then the ozone may go and flip and we all get buried under some fool glacier? Or even if there is no big bang, there's no mark, no record to be made anyway, because in much less than even a thousand years no one's givin' a shit. Everybody's wound up bein' drug addicts. We went and lost the war on drugs and couldn't care less about anything but gettin' high. Or maybe, we all pack it in gettin' eaten up by AIDS."

"Glad to know you're prepared, Oscar. You have not only thought your way through every existential possibility, you have also considered every contingency, and each and every state of being and of non-being."

"Fancy words, Adam. Those are just highbrow, high fallutin', empty, meaningless words. And I don't have any ideas at all about non-bein'. When I see someone who is dead, I have no way of knowin' what his or her state is.

I don't know anything about such conditions. And there is no point to my even wonderin' about it. Where's it gonna get me? When my time comes, I'll know soon enough."

"Then, there's no getting to know anything."

"You can't be sure of that. But if it's so, so be it and so what?"

Something about Oscar's manner puzzled Adam. Was it that his air of frustration had left him? Was Oscar getting security enough from his new appointment to quell his sense of urgency for making it big? Or, was he tending now to see his own difficulty in the broader sense of black people's in general and ready to settle for the same sacrificial fate under discrimination as had been endured by so many of his crusading forebears?

There was one other odd thing about this unexpected and hurried visit from Oscar. When Oscar left, they simply parted. No hand shake. No bear hug. No meaningfully loaded eyeings. And also, no further mention of the book. It was as if, suddenly, Adam was no longer recruited. Or had he been given, quite craftily, some kind of a free hand? To let his own conscience be his guide?

Twenty-two

A fter three dragging days it was time finally to check on Charlene's progress. Adam dialed the number. The phone rang a very long while, but there was no answer. She was probably out shopping. After all, it was mid-morning and up until now he had only called at night. Around noon, he dialed again. This time, on the third ring, there was a voice but a strange one. It was a recorded announcement. The number was out of service.

This could be a bother. Obviously, she had neglected to pay the phone bill in spite of having all that money, and now they'd cut her off. He'd never gone to her place without calling the night before and being expected. Adam didn't take to the idea of going over there and winding up in the lobby, pushing unavailingly against the buzzer, Charlene happening still to be out somewhere.

It was annoying also for another reason. When he'd awakened, it was with longing. He wished, of course, to see what she'd accomplished during the last three days but also there was this urgency. It had been building during the time of their separation and was now a dilemma. What was to come of it both today and over the long run? After all, Charlene was only supposed to be a passing fancy. When their affair would be over, would his craving obligingly ease off? Or would he be driven elsewhere to satisfy it? Neither prospect was appealing. And looking elsewhere for women was not practical, either in his circumstance or at his age. Hard to see himself cruising the singles bar scene. So much consternation, all because a little sex play had seemed to moderate his depression. Not an especially good situation to have come to a head on the very last day the phone bill was due.

It would soon be too late in the day if he didn't get going, whatever the situation happened to be with her phone. So Adam drove over to her place and dutifully pressed the outside buzzer. No familiar welcoming voice came over the intercom and there was no upbeat chatter of electrical release for the lock in the lobby door. Was she now in the bathroom? Or still out shopping? Or gone downtown, actually, to pay the phone bill? He saw a man cutting grass out front.

"Didn't happen to see Miss Davis, did you?"

"Wouldn't know her if I saw her, mister. They is always comin' and goin' 'round here. I don't bother much with anybody but the super."

"Where's he?"

"Gone to the hardware store. Needed a flush valve for a toilet. He'll be back in a while."

"Look, I'll take a short walk. When I'm back, think he can let me wait for her inside?"

"Hell, I don't know nothin' 'bout that. I just cut the grass and mind my own damned business. But I sure don't think he's gonna' let you up in her apartment."

Right then, being elsewhere, if only to be cutting grass himself, was starting to look real good to Adam. He could just about see himself behind his own mower, in his own backyard, fenced away from all of this convoluted conniving, and just like this lawn man, be minding his "own damned business". How had he gotten himself exposed so badly? How had he wandered into this strange and foreign sort of world? He wasn't even sure anymore that Oscar still wanted him to go ahead with the book.

He made several turns around the block. After the last one, the lawn man beckoned him over.

"He's back."

"Where's he at?"

"Gone inside. Jus' ring his bell."

Adam approached the entrance once more, but before summoning anyone else he pressed the button to 5C DAVIS. No answer. He worked the button for SUPERINTENDENT.

"Who's that?"

"A friend of Davis in 5C. I'd like to wait for her in the lobby."

"No point to it. She ain't here."

There was an unpleasant sensation in mid-abdomen, something like a jab. Also a drawing in his calf muscles.

"Not here?" Adam called into question the man's blanket assertion. "You mean out of town or just out?"

"Hell, man. Gone. I mean disappeared. Skipped. Vamoosed. You figure it out for yourself. If I was to be wonderin' at all the comin's and goin's 'round here without so much as a hello or goodbye, I wouldn't have time for anything else."

One well intended and nobly inspired literary project

was turned sudden nightmare. Was he about to collapse? Getting this queasy, this fast, might not take so well for a person of his years. He feared for his heart but the weight seemed at the back of his neck, not across the chest. Quick further self-assessment revealed wobbly knees, somewhat quick respirations, and the calf muscle aberration had now become a steady painful tightness. Should he just run for it? Duck for home? If on the verge of succumbing to this shock, he would be a damned sight better off there than winding up passed out on the corner of 16th and Columbia. Even dropping dead behind the wheel was more accept-able than to be found around here without explanation, or even worse, begging one that could be easily guessed at. Funny, or better, not really funny but weird. He had never had apprehensions before this for dropping dead in the neighborhood. Even on Charlene's mattress he hadn't. Sex, for sure, was one hell of a reality blinding imperative, but wasn't it though. But sex had no sway here now. This was about survival.

Yet just short of bolting, Adam was able to muster some reserves. Hard pressed by an intruding need to know why all of this was happening to him, and hoping still to find an answer other than the obvious, he quizzed the superintendent further.

"How about a forwarding address?"

Only to be slapped down.

"Nothin' buddy."

"Look. She had stuff that belonged to me, papers, tapes, records. Any possibility something was left behind?"

"Wait a minute."

After not one, but several dawdling minutes, the lobby door was opened by a pleasant looking black man in tidy khaki uniform. The fellow appeared to be about Adam's age. That was nice, kind of reassuring. Made it easier to confide in him, if need be. Maybe now, Adam was even breathing a little better. The super crooked a finger at him wordlessly and led him to the elevator. Up on five, he used his pass key to unlock her door giving entry to a cold and barren place. What had been there to make it somewhat genial was no more. Adam was at a loss and under the stress of having suffered one hell of a big one at that.

"Shit! She took everything."

"Not her, buddy. It was some rental company came in here to grab it all. They said she was more than three months behind."

"What about the rent? The landlord get his money?"

"Not after the first month, he didn't. Never saw a dime from that gal after that. Always puttin' him off."

"So she broke the lease?"

"Lease? We got no leases 'round here. Everythin's on month to month."

Adam, having trouble with his mouth and throat, went for water.

"They're here!"

"Whatcha got, mister?"

"Out here in the kitchen. All my material. The tapes and other things."

Every bit of it was there. The essence of Oscar Brown Jr. was strewn across the top of a dishwasher. Such relief to have it back in hand and yet he resented her crude and rough rejection of it. The gall she'd had to toss it about so. But what could really be expected from a flim flam artist? Sensitivity? He recalled his recent urge to throttle her. Had it been unerring instinct? Instinct that took better measure of her than the amateurish finagler who'd usurped his brain and was blind to her duplicity?

"Important stuff, mister?"

"Only to me."

"Well you are damned lucky then. I always had the feelin' that dame would just about pick your bones clean for anything worth nibblin' on. She was a smooth one though. And real educated, too, I guess. You don't get her kind of high and fancy airs without havin' learned somethin' 'sides what you do in the streets. But I guess she put her time in there, also."

"Why do you say that?"

"'Cause time an' again I'd see her hangin' out with this real sneaky and sharp lookin' dude. She'd meet him right outside the front door of this place. Never took him inside though. Then he'd be off like a shot. Guys from the rental company said they weren't even sure Davis was her right name. Yep, she was a highbrow kind'a trickster. But tell me, mister. How come a straight lookin' solid enough man like you gets himself mixed up with her kind of woman? Them good looks of hers got to yuh, hey?"

"I hired her to do some typing for me."

"And the one thing led to the other, right?"

Now the obliging superintendent was snickering. Adam was not about to admit to anything. This was not, after all, an old timers' true confessions sort of thing. He stayed on track, careful not to make the other a bona fide confidante.

"She never got it done."

Nor commenced, for that matter, if the truth were to be told. But since the truth had never been started up on ever since Charlene had come upon the scene, it was kind of late for declaring it now.

"Well mister, maybe now you'll stay clear of these fast-track modern dames. Whooee, they are somethin' else these days. Just leave me to my old lady, if you please. I don't do no messin' 'round with any of them other kind. I like things plain, straight, and simple. Know what I mean? Are we all through here now?"

"You can say that again."

"Okay then. I'm lockin' it up."

Adam gathered together what he'd been lucky enough to retrieve, slipped his accommodating companion a ten dollar bill for his trouble, and left.

Whenever things turned sour for Adam, he would come up with formulas for regrouping but precede them always with a single self-directed question: Might it have been worse? Driving home that early afternoon, it was no different.

Why sure. The tapes could be gone and wind up almost anywhere with unaccountable consequences, even misfortune. Every last bit of the kruggerand money might gradually have been eased from him. Or horror of horrors, Clare could have found out everything. And who knows what kind of grief that mysterious guy whom Charlene (or whatever her name was) had hanging around outside, might eventually have brought down on him. No, a person could even say he was getting off rather well. Was he not also pointed safely home now and toward a place where he had every right, from here on in, to just sit around and do nothing but settle for what comforts he had? In fact, in some ways, he should even feel more pity than anger for Charlene (or whoever she was). She, for all her skullduggery, would probably never know much in the way of good fortune. And God, but wasn't she a sexy piece and for that, anyway, hadn't he joy to remember?

By the time he was home, Adam, if not fully restored, was at least in working order. Just as well because if he was to have concerns at all from here on in, they'd best be directed at what needed to be done about Oscar's book. Now it was all up to him. His evasive gambit was over and done with.

Twenty-three

Days passed. Adam knew what was needed, but something was lacking. There had been no problem in sitting down before the computer and taking his first stabs at it. He'd even explained to Clare that now the book had fallen entirely to him because "Miss Davis had been called out of town through sickness in her family." So no explanation was required for him to be sitting at the machine. What required explanation to Clare, however, and insight for him, was why he wasn't coming up with anything. Every start, after but a few lines, got him nowhere. He'd be left suspended, staring into empty taunting space above the monitor or looking out the window or at his dogs sprawled alongside him.

If Oscar's key call was his song, "Brother Where Are You?," this question was easily answered. He was right there, sitting at that computer, and stalled. Unfortunately, for some peculiar reason, Adam's spirit or mind or both were not moving him to get his brotherly job done. Clare was discerning if not particularly helpful.

"Another bad morning? Maybe, instead of typing, you should just straight out dictate."

"I considered that. No good. I can bear with the sound of my thoughts but not my actual voice."

"How wild. Whatever made you say that?"

"I guess it's because I don't really like myself. It's easy, pretty much to avoid the sight of me. Impossible, though, not to hear me once I start sounding off. Remember when I used to play back my office dictation so I could make corrections? I could barely wait to get it over with. Hated, absolutely hated the sound of my voice. So how could I possibly talk my way through an entire book? I'd wind up in that nut house you fancy so much. Anyway, that's not where the problem is. It's not in the mechanics of writing. It's in the conception. I'm drawing a blank and I'm beginning to wonder if it's because when I think about Oscar's music or his lyrics, I don't seem to get turned on. It's hard, otherwise, to understand why I can't get myself stirred up enough so as to be productive. These days, even playing his records doesn't do anything for me. The sad thing is, up until now, not only did his performances always move me, but as I told you, one of the reasons for still doing the book was that I wanted everyone else to get the same kind of pleasure I'd had. Figure that one out."

"Perhaps you just need a vacation."

"From what? The whole rest of my life stands to be a vacation. I can't see any point in spending a bunch of money only to be hanging out somewhere else and be thinking about this infernal machine back here and what needs to be tapped into it. Anyway, weren't you the first to ask, what do I know about this kind of writing? So that's probably it. How, all of a sudden do I figure to come off as a red hot biographer?"

"You are just looking for reasons to drop the whole thing."

"Yeah? Well there's no problem in finding some damned good ones."

And yet, for all their arguing, Adam accommodated Clare's insistence that he remain at his station in hope of gaining some biographical momentum.

Twenty-four

It was the fourth morning of futile posturing before his machine and Clare had gone out to shop. Adam and the dogs were in their usual locations and in their just about well matched, mindless modes. When the phone rang, he welcomed it as a reprieve from this enduring vacancy. He didn't even care that when he got up a bit too rapidly from his chair, he happened to trip and strike his head rather soundly against the fortunately well-padded back surface of a nearby couch. It was enough of a blow, though, to momentarily stun him and set him up for another.

"May I please speak to Adam Grossman?"

"Who's this?"

"Tim McMann. Head of security at the Watergate Hotel. That you, doc?"

"Yes sir."

"How you doin', doc? I remember when you used to be one of our old time, steady customers around here, down in the health club. Haven't seen you for years. Where you been?"

"Nowhere. I just quit all that swimming and jog with my dogs now. Or work out on my Nordic Track up in the bedroom. What's up, Mr. McMann?"

"You know a Charlene Davis? Says she knows you."

Although still a bit shaky from the effects of his fall, Adam could still manage, nevertheless, to quickly figure out that to be credible, he had to answer just as fast. And certainly he wanted to declare almost instantly, "Hell no." But if he sounded either too emphatic or too quick, the contrary truth would be out just as soon and obviously as if he were to hesitate. No use. Any opportunity for cover up was gone. There was no way to mastermind a perfectly paced disclaimer. He yielded to the inevitable. For better or for worse, he was stuck with the kind of truth that for good reason was called awful. It was a strange combination that, Charlene, he, and a thing called truth. He was also being taken at that moment with the worst of those god awful sensations in his chest, abdomen, and legs, yet to have come from knowing this eventful woman.

"Sure I know her. She have some kind of a problem?"

More to the point, what sort of vexation was she standing to bring down on him now?

"Could be. She checked in here a few days ago. Had no credit card, but put down a big cash deposit. Left her departure date open-ended. Ran up quite a bill with all kinds of room service. Even went to our top restaurant, you know the one, Jean-Louis. She's a real sharp-looking woman. Well you've probably noticed that yourself. But, for me, she just didn't seem to fit in, so me and my men have been keeping an eye on her. Well today she trots herself through the lobby carrying a suitcase, heads for a cab, and doesn't turn in her room key or pay the bill, so we nabbed her, and whatcha know? Her room was clean emptied out."

Adam was oddly resentful. He didn't like McMann's snooty suggestion that Charlene "didn't seem to fit in." The guy was obviously a racist, and Adam wouldn't mind telling him he'd be positively proud to be seen with Charlene anywhere, including at Jean-Louis. As far as he was concerned, Charlene was downright elegant.

"She did a lot of typing for me."

The truth, quite obviously, would need a little working around, if this situation was to get straightened out.

"Yeah? Well now she is screaming bloody murder at us about false detention. Also says she had no plan to check out for a few more days. What she was doing with her clothes was taking them to a dry cleaner. Christ, we've got a helluva good one right here in the hotel. Then she flashes this big wad of dough at us, claiming her intention all along was to pay her bill when she was damned good and ready and out of that. Then she counts out more than four grand just to show us what she's got, and says she knows you and that you will vouch for her. Says you even gave her all that cash. So what's the deal, doc?"

Time, at long last, for the truth? Or yet another tricky variant of it? He had no choice, but how much more confusion of fact would be required to extricate himself from this new predicament? And should he not do Charlene's bidding and convey the anticipated "vouching for," what might be her terrible retaliation? After all, her gorgeous back was right up against a very inhospitable Watergate wall. For Adam, right now, even a little uncertainty could be very intimidating, and he was feeling a monstrous lot of it.

"She's right. I gave her the money."

"Doc. All that dough in cash?"

Adam was inclined now to get his own back up a little. Since when was cash illegal? He hadn't exactly printed it himself. In fact, he was rather proud of his connivance to make it the modus operandi for his dealings with Charlene. The nerve of this fellow McMann. He was supposed to be a security agent, not a point man for the IRS. And even if he were with Internal Revenue, electronic banking or no, cash was still the coin of the realm. Anyway, he'd try to explain it all quite fully.

"Look. She did some typing and other kinds of paperwork for me and wanted cash. That was what she asked me for and I certainly had no reason to refuse her. With her not being a regular salaried employee, there was no income tax to be withheld, so what she did with the money, or about reporting it as an earning, was entirely up to her. And cash or no, it was still a legitimate itemized business deduction for me."

So there. Who could ask for a better explanation than that?

"You know where she was living, doc?"

"Well, she's from out of town. She had a temporary place, I think, over on Columbia Road. Last time I saw her I really didn't know where she might be heading next."

That was for sure.

"Damn it, doc, I guess we screwed up on this one. I just hope she doesn't think of suing us. Right now though she is sure yelling her head off. Never in all my years have I run into something like this one."

Neither had Adam and he had a lot more years on him than McMann.

"I still can't figure out why she has to head for an

outside cleaner. Ours is not that expensive. But you sure don't arrest people for something like that. Boy though, did she ever have her dresses jammed into that bag. And you know what, doc? She hasn't got a single nightgown. Then there's the other thing. She's also yelling about improper search, invasion of her privacy, you name it. Hell. Lucky we called you before we went and got the cops."

"Really screaming, is she?"

"Yeah. You better know it. Say doc, you wouldn't have time to come by and sort of help us smooth this situation over, would you?"

"I'll be right down. With the parkway, it'll take about fifteen minutes."

Yet again, a thing with no alternative.

Twenty-five

A dam was not your aggressive sort of driver. With him behind the wheel, passengers and following drivers alike were usually confounded by his irritating tendency to poke along or meander. Today was different. He fairly flew down Beach Drive, then Rock Creek Parkway, making it in twelve minutes flat. Parking in the underground garage and stairs to the hotel lobby were also negotiated at an unprecedented breakneck speed. McMann was waiting for him.

"Hi doc. You're looking good."

"Where's Charlene?"

"Back up in 1226."

"How do you know that?"

"Well, it's where we left her. And she sure ain't going out for any dry cleaning. For amends, we had the concierge take all her dresses and we're gonna get it done for free by our own cleaner."

Adam imagined her, anyway, sneaking down the backstairs and heading for an exit other than the one in front.

"She know I was on my way down here?"

"No, doc. I figured it better not to let on we were asking you to do it. Didn't want it to look any worse than it might seem already. Know what I mean?"

"I suppose so."

"And doc, anytime you want to come back and use the health club, don't hesitate. It's on the house."

"Thanks. I'll head upstairs."

As he stepped off the elevator, Adam was going over his motives for coming downtown. They weren't just about getting back at her. They were also about resolving a mystery and maybe even seeing a return of some of his money. To these things, he felt entitled. 1226 was right across the hall.

Once again he was back to operating a buzzer.

No answer from inside, but he'd heard a footstep, a TV being switched off, and possibly seen a shadow quickly becoming none as it backed away from the peep hole in the door. He pressed the buzzer once more.

"C'mon, Charlene. I know you're in there. I'm only here to talk."

At once the door cracked open and there was that bountiful gal.

"Adam."

"You going to ask me in? Or are you particular about whom you hang out with now that you've moved up in the world?"

She looked a little frayed and he felt sorry for having said that.

"You don't have to be mean, Adam."

He entered what was more suite than room, and walked about. "Let's see. Aren't we sumptuous though? Nice little kitchen and dining area, sitting room, balcony on the river, private sleeping alcove and big king-sized bed. Or is it a queen model? Ought to be for a grand girl like you, right, Charlene?"

"What's wrong with me livin' nice for a change? I'm a person too, you know."

"On money you stole from me and still owed a lot of other people?"

"You're a real stickler for irrelevant details, Adam. Nobody's been deprived of anything they'd miss one darn bit."

"Irrelevant, Charlene? Is that what everybody else's pain is?"

"There's not anyone hurtin' unless they talk themselves into it."

"I keep calling you Charlene. That's not even your real name, is it?"

"I hope to tell you it is."

"But Charlene Davis is a writer, a published writer. And you're nothing but a full time crook."

"Let's just say I'm a different Charlene Davis. There are lots of us with the same slave name. Get it, Adam? Just a coincidence. That's all. The other Charlene Davis really is a writer. This one isn't and she has fallen onto hard times. You've heard about the recession, or haven't you Adam? Look, I appreciate your backing me up with the security guys. I figured that even with all that money on me, or maybe only because I had so much, without someone like you to vouch for me I'd wind up in the can. So I owe you for that. Once more, I owe you, okay? And I'm sorry I conned you. That's it. Take it or leave it. It's all I have to say."

"And the money?"

"After I pay the tab here, you can take the lot. There's

plenty left. I just don't give a damn anymore. So, can we get off it now? That's unless you've got some kinky kind of thing for dishin' out pain."

Adam remembered again that urge to wring her tempting neck, but it wasn't with him now.

"Mind answering just a few simple questions?"

They repositioned themselves, almost simultaneously, from being faced off to sitting in chairs angled in opposite directions.

"Nope. Fire away, massuh. After all, I've been well caught, but ain't I though?" said she to an indifferent ceiling and wall.

"What in hell were you up to when you went to Oscar's show at the Barry Theater, and tapped me on the shoulder for the big come on?"

"Well, I'd been hearin' about Oscar Brown Jr., for years and years, but never seen him. So, when I saw the ad in the paper sayin' he was comin' to town, I just went down and bought myself a ticket. Once inside, I started to figure wouldn't it be neat if maybe somehow I could get in tight with his crowd, you know, at least for awhile. So I decided to just up and proposition him about doin' some kind of a write-up. Sort of trade on the rep', if he knew her, of my namesake, Charlene Davis, the writer. Then along came this dude, Adam, who from all appearances, looked like an even better ticket for runnin' with Oscar's bunch. What with the way you knew them all, Oscar, his family, the musicians, it looked like a perfect set-up. And then of all the crazy things, almost right off the bat, you wanta' hire me to do this book deal. So everything went from there."

"I'm not sure I go for any of this. It's too pat. You are probably a pathological liar."

"Suit yourself, Adam. It's a free country. Anyway, for thems that have, it is."

"What kind of scams were you working before you got inspired to pull this one off?"

"Listen man, I've always been a good little girl. I just have a terrific imagination, that's all. So sometimes I pass myself off for somethin' I'm not. So what? I never hurt anybody by it. I'd just do it to live a little, for a change. That's all. Then, when I came to Washington and couldn't get a decent job... Hell, I'm a damned college graduate. I'm supposed to be out there, gettin' to do stuff in public relations. How'd you like to be in a situation like that? And Adam, you think that Oscar is so cool, don't you, when he sings about bein' broke or gettin' busted? Well, maybe it's all a big joke and so many catchy tunes for rich and privileged people like you all, but it sure ain't that way for us sisters and brothers close to bein' really down and out and in the streets."

Adam had still other questions needing answers.

"What about that guy hanging around your front door?"

"That too? You spotted Leroy, did you? Ain't you the old fox. Look, I don't drink. So what harm is there if I relax a little once in awhile with some pot? Big fuckin' deal."

"If you were only after my money, once you had it, why in hell come to a swank place like this where you'd have to part with at least some of it before you could finally take off? Why not just disappear?"

"No more than dumb impulse. That's all. I think maybe you were really responsible for that. And don't think I was only after your money. I resent that."

"What in hell are you saying now?"

"Look, Adam. For only a few days and before I split for who knows where, I wanted to feel big-time fancy like you and your kinda people. So what's fancier than the Watergate Hotel? Not much, I guess. Bein' with you, gave me a taste, maybe even a need for somethin' like that. And bein' with you gave me other kinds of problems, too, especially when I knew I couldn't lead you on much longer about this dumb writin' deal and I had to start plannin' my getaway."

"You were afraid I'd turn you in, call the police?"

"Hell no. I guess I'll never stop wondering about your head, Adam. Is it like always, up there somewhere in the clouds? Talk about bein' spaced out. Look, I've got no way of knowin' how it is or used to be between you and your old lady. I just know that you and I had it great. But you are forever so damned locked in to stuff that counts for just about nothin', lookin' back on it all, I don't think it ever dawned on you, not even one single time with us, that you might very well be in bed for the very last damned second in your ever lovin', hung-up, senior citizen kinda life with someone who enjoyed you like gangbusters, and who also really dug you big time. For me, that was one helluva problem."

"Dug me?"

"You want I should say it some other way?"

This was indeed a mad scene. Luxury suite at the Watergate Hotel at mid-day. Wife Clare, off to the Safeway. The dogs lying around back home, and maybe wondering when someone was going to show up and put them out. And he, a sixty-six-year-old former cardiac surgeon, recently turned aspiring biographer, seated opposite a young and beautiful, barely black woman, who had shacked up with him, robbed him, lied to him, and now, all of a sudden, was intimating she more than "dug" him. How crazy did the next scene stand to be? Maybe he'd better beat it out of there well before it started. And yet, for all of Adam's current uncertainty and anxiety, this tidy, decorous, dead quiet hotel room, looking out to a dull gray sky and the dead calm Potomac, was tranquilizing.

"You had any breakfast, Charlene?"

"Nope."

"Want some lunch?"

"What you thinkin' of?"

"Well, they tell me you're hot for ordering up room service. At least, that's what I hear from the management."

"Don't get nasty, Adam, and don't smart ass me."

"I'm going to call down for a steak sandwich. What'll you have?"

"Same, but real well done."

"Something to drink?"

"No thanks. There's still some cokes from last night over in the fridge."

"Maybe the occasion calls for wine."

"I said I don't drink. What you leadin' up to?"

"Okay, I'll just make it a half bottle for me. That'll save you quite some dough."

"It's your money, not mine."

"I haven't gotten it back yet, as best I recall."

Charlene rose and went to her purse which was resting on top a chest of drawers. She extracted an envelope tightly packed with his hundred dollar bills and tossed it across the room where it landed on the bed."

"You're short maybe four hundred."

"You're very welcome."

Charlene smiled, laughed, then began to cry.

"Please, Charlene..."

"Oh just shut up, Adam. I thought you were gonna' order us up some food."

He reached for the phone and did it. Then they just sat facing each other for several minutes, Adam thoughtful, Charlene spent.

"I better call home or I'll be reported a missing person."

"Must be nice havin' someone to worry where you are."

Adam dialed his number. Clare picked up.

"I'm downtown on business."

"What kind of business?"

"Been talking to that lawyer I told you about. You know, the one with the malpractice suit against our friend?"

"I guess there's no use warning you about anything, Adam. You're always going to do what you're driven to do. But the poor man's got AIDS, hasn't he? So how can they go ahead and sue him?"

"It doesn't make any difference. It doesn't even matter whether or not he's still around when the case goes to court. There's insurance coverage and that's all the lawyers ever care about. So I think I'll be awhile. Maybe even quite late. This guy is so overwhelmed I'm even considering to as much as look at the medical records, he wants to take me out to dinner."

When Adam was through with the phone he found Charlene in a state of open mouthed incredulity.

"Look who's been callin' whom a liar."

"Why do you say that? Every bit of what you heard has real or impending substance. Maybe not if you take it all together, but each and every one of those statements has the ring of gospel."

"So you're a smarter liar than me. Big deal. You've had more time to polish your act."

The doorbell rang. Adam tipped the waiter and they were into their meal, each being seated at opposite ends of a small dining table on which their order had been set. Adam ate tidily, cutting into his steak with precision and seeming to savor the wine. Charlene's attack upon her meal was exactly that. It was executed with gusto.

"You know, Charlene, it just occurred to me, we've never eaten together before. And I kind of like this formal touch. Don't you? Damned if we aren't sitting here like the lord and lady of the manor."

"I can't afford to be a snob. I'll leave that to you and your folks. And stop talkin' down to me, Adam. I don't appreciate it."

"You said you dug me."

"That's different. I just hate bein' held low or bein' abused by anyone. But at least you're not raisin' a hand to me. Considerin' all that's happened, there's lots of men who'd do just that, they'd be bangin' me around considerably."

"Suppose I admitted there was a time I felt like choking you to death."

"Really, Adam?"

"Really."

"That's wonderful."

"Wonderful?"

"Oh shut up."

In an instant she vaulted and was all over him. Stepping quickly around the table, she raised her skirt so as to straddle his lap, with thighs and legs encircling both him and his chair so effectively he could barely move anything but his arms. And they were just about useless save to topple limply around her waist. Her kisses virtually robbed him of air, and she was at it for so long he had the distinct impression these kisses were of a duration exceeding the sum total of all those received previously. At last, she did stop, leaned back, and smiled down at him.

"It is a terrific bed, you know. Much better than that lumpy old mattress we had. Want to try it? Want to screw me again, Adam?"

"You finished with your steak?"

"Sure thing, honey man."

"You know, if we go and do it, I still won't be sure, for certain, exactly who it is I'm in bed with."

"Trust me, Adam. You definitely will."

"Well that might make it kind of special."

Because Adam did have that sense, it was their best ever. And because he was not constrained by the habitual clock watching that had gone with their previous joinings, there was no need, afterward, for him to do anything but to linger and reflect on his pleasure. That bit of reverie was broken only by a call to security to say that "Miss Davis was being quite gracious and was willing to forget the entire matter of her unreasonable detention and harassment."

Charlene had managed to work a remarkable and quick change in his perspective. It certainly had to do with how well they had come together in bed. More importantly, though, with only a few impetuous but well-targeted words, she had drawn him back full circle to his much earlier mullings. This predictably ill-fated love of theirs, that of an older man for a young woman, met perfectly

the required test. More than any other fragile and imper-
manent arrangement he might incline to savor, there were
none so imminently poised to dissolve as their union. When
Charlene insisted he was stupid for not ever having had
the high probability "even dawn" upon him that she was
his very last ticket to real rapture, that's when Adam saw
the light. Without realizing it, for all of those sex-filled
weeks at her place, his astrophysically derived postulation
was being joyfully proven.

"Adam, do I hear you hummin' or is there somethin'
runnin' in the bath room?"

"It's me, sweetie."

"Sweetie? Why. that's nice."

"Yes, and what I'm humming are a few lines Oscar
used to sing."

"Solid. I kinda missed not hearin' old Oscar's sing-
along while we were into all our heavy breathin'. How
does it go?"

"Well, what I'm remembering are lines from just one
song. It was about being lucky, damned lucky."

"And that's how you're feelin' now?"

"Correct Charlene, correct."

How could it be otherwise? How many fellows his age
had such a gorgeous girl, a loving, understanding wife,
free time, health, income, home, dogs, boat, all kinds of
other security and to boot, had figured out their only way
to enjoy life in the last years left them? Probably damned
few, if any.

"What are we goin' to do, Adam?"

"You mean about dinner?"

"No, you old jerk. About us."

"Well I need to rest a few minutes before I take another

crack at it. You've got me scared with all that stuff about it being maybe my last."

"That's not what I mean, either. I mean where do we, or rather I, go from here?"

"Well first, I'm going to help you spend some of that money we had to dump on the floor when we hit the sheets."

"Really? Whatcha gonna' buy me?"

"Now we mustn't start all over again on being that kinda' girl. I'll probably never buy you anything. You and I have to be practical about this love of ours."

"Love, Adam?"

"Yeah, not dig, love. I'm a little more daring than you are, kiddo."

"Wow."

He was rewarded with a somewhat different kind of kiss, one with all sorts of possible implications.

"We are going out to shop, but not for anything trivial. We've got to conserve our resources but we are going to make a cash deposit on a nice little furnished efficiency right across from the Watergate. And I am going to rejoin the Watergate Health Club so we can be neighbors, kissing kinds of neighbors. Get it?"

"When did you think this all up? And then what?"

"It came to me in a rare moment of, shall I say, excitatory revelation. 'Then what' is that I will get you a job."

"Doing what?"

"You say you have a degree, but I know you can't write. The question is, can you type?"

"Sure. Real good."

"Well, my only condition on being an expert witness for this very big-deal malpractice attorney, and a case like his will drag on for years and years, will be that he find a place for you in his office, and at a decent salary. And you know where that office happens to be?"

"Right here, right?"

"Correct. Next door in the Watergate office building."

"Adam, you're a genius."

"No, you're the genius, Charlene. After all, it was you who led me back to the Watergate. It was you who decided this was the place to rip off. Just so that right here I could get reoriented and become downright inspired."

"Okay, okay. It's a real cool idea. I'm for it. I'm for it. No. I love it. I love it."

"Here comes the best part."

"Stop right there, Adam. My little heart can't take any more. You come up with any more big ideas and it's me, not you, who is going to drop dead. You're gettin' to be much too much for me."

"Now I can write the book about Oscar. I can do it. No question about it."

"That'd be somethin' else. I really admire that man."

"Yes, but not as a biography. I won't do it that way."

"What other way is there?"

"I can try to put myself in his shoes, Charlene, and have Oscar tell his own story. Maybe no one else should presume to tell it, anyway. It might sound too phony. Of course, it would be a pseudo-autobiography. But God knows, for all these years, I've been hearing nothing else out of him but 'I did this,' or 'I did that.' He's been telling it to me often enough all along. He's always saying what he did, what he wrote, where he performed, and how he's been shafted. It's a natural. I'll fall right into it. Or you know, it might be told kind of like they did back in Africa, the word getting passed along from person to person, generation to generation, among different people, each putting his own spin on it. That's another way to do it, with a bunch of narrators."

"Blockbuster, Adam. Absolute blockbuster."

"And you know why I can pull it off now?"

"Beats me. There's just no second guessin' or even keepin' up with you anymore."

"Well, I can't ever be black but because of you I'm a helluva lot closer to Oscar Brown Jr., than I've ever been before. I've crossed over the damned line also. We did it together, you and me."

"Adam, that's terrible. I do believe you're plannin' to use me. What a switch."

"Yes, but aren't we having fun? Isn't it a super trip? And you know something else? Out of the entire universe, I've come up with the biggest and best damned actual bang that could ever hit on me. The only kind that really stands to count."

"Adam, you're the baddest of the bad."

"By the way."

"What now, hon'?"

"You wouldn't happen to have some pot stashed away, would you? It'd come in handy with this new approach of mine."

"Let's do it."

Twenty-six

Not quite how it turned out. Adam did set up a small studio apartment for Charlene and she got the secretarial job. He seemed to live an enlivened double life, even motivated to work steadily on the book. But then, once again, Charlene was gone. This time, at least, she left a note: "Sorry, Adam. Got a better deal."

Nonetheless he owed her. For by then the writing had acquired its own momentum and in spite of the fact Charlene was no longer there, he had to follow through on the book, as much to make good on his earlier boasting to Charlene as to do his friend Oscar a presumably well-deserved good turn.

He was quite single minded about the necessary labors, allowing himself no distractions at all, until at last, the job was done. Only when he dreamed did he seem to engage the unpleasant implications of his new isolation. Like on the night he finished the last page, he dreamed that he was still at his computer pressing his finger down over and over again upon the DELETE key. What would he now opt to do away with?

Twice he read the manuscript through. Satisfied, he express mailed a copy to Oscar who was still in Los Angeles.

Three days later, Oscar called.

"Have you looked it over?"

"No time. No time, man. Too busy jus' stayin' alive. Adam, I really need two grand right away. We are behind with the rent and the landlord is startin' to make noises."

"What's going on with the job?'

"Cancelled without so much as a 'so sorry.' Look, I'm due a gig end of the month. Pay you back right afterward."

Adam could recall other times he'd gotten such promises, all turning out to be quite empty. "Pay back" was beyond the means of some one living hand to mouth.

"Okay, but read the book."

"Gotcha. Thanks Adam."

Hearing nothing further from L.A., Adam made his own call two weeks later.

"Oscar, have you read it?'

"Well, not entirely."

"No good?"

"It's a drag, man. I gave up on it."

"How's that?"

"Jesus Christ, Adam. How'd you like to be up against it and have to read that you're a fuckin' failure? You got any idea what kinda' trip that is for someone gaspin' for air? It sucks, man. It just plain sucks."

"That is not how I wrote it. What I'm describing is a guy with real talent, who is owed a helluva lot more credit than he's ever gotten. This book is all about him being, an unrecognized musical and lyrical genius. Now you knew all along that was the angle both of us laid out for this thing right from the get go. That was our clear understanding. And it was also to point up what you are currently having to go through."

"An' you've got me whinin' and complainin'. I never complain."

"Maybe I dialed the wrong number. This Oscar Brown Jr.?"

"An' besides which, if you really wanted to lend a hand you could damned sure do a helluva lot more than write some stupid book."

"Like what, for instance?"

"Well, how much time you figure you put in on all a' this?"

"Maybe six, seven, hours a day the last eight months or so."

"Yeah? Well I'd be a damned sight better off if insteada' all a' that you'd spent the time doin' somethin' really useful like jus' pickin' up the phone and tryin' to get me some gigs. Imagine where we might be if you'da spent all those hours on the phone 'steada sittin' around writin' me up for some kinda' fuckin' has been."

"Christ, Oscar. We've been through all of that a dozen times. I am not and do not know how to be anybody's personal agent."

"Well you obviously ain't no writer either and that didn't seem to stop you none. Why do one thing and not the other? You say you're my friend, but I don't see you even tryin'."

"Thanks a lot."

"You wouldn't publish this thing without my permission, would you?"

"Of course not. Why would I do something like that?"

"Well let's just see that you don't. Listen, I gotta make some calls. I'll get back to you."

As far as Adam was concerned, Oscar needn't bother. Not even with the two thousand dollars. He could keep it. Just let him go away and stay away. Period.

"Was all of that what I think it was?"

Clare had been right there, in the next room, listening.

"Correct. Oscar has changed his mind. He's turning down the book and says I'm no friend of his."

Adam was silent for several moments then resumed. "You know babe, there's a psychiatrist in Bethesda advocating total honesty. Says it's the only way to go. What do you think about that?"

"We aren't suited to blabbing everything that crosses our minds."

"Why not? That could be the real intimacy people are always hankering for."

"Listen Adam, if I knew every one of your crazy schemes and thoughts, some night I might grab one of your old scalpels and slit your throat. Let's just keep this relationship of ours like it is, a complete mystery. Trust me. It's safer that way for both of us. What's this all about, anyway?"

"Well, it's true confession time. You remember Charlene Davis? She was back here for awhile. Actually, she never left. We managed to get it on pretty good for several weeks but then she finally did take off. That damned gal really cost me."

"This is all supposed to be some kind of a secret?"

"You knew?"

"Let's just say it wouldn't take much of a guess. So

Adam, now that you've gotten it off your chest, are you feeling better for all of this intimacy?"

"And for my money, which is also an apt way to put it, Oscar Brown Jr. is a self-centered, egotistical ingrate."

"But a fabulous entertainer. So Adam, for God's sake, just don't hang out with him. Settle for playing his records. Or sneak into the theater without him ever knowing you're there."

"You are absolutely right. You know Clare, you are truly remarkable. Without you, this would be a real empty place."

"Well what's on your agenda next? What can I expect from you?"

"You mean like do something, like really do something?"

"Sure. You know. The way you've always put it. Make your mark."

"No more of that. I've given up on it. I'm goin' to just lay around and maybe have myself a little ordinary low keyed irrelevant fun for a change. And try to be a sort of, you know, decent, and up front kinda' guy. Make my mark? And meanwhile the whole damned universe is getting ready to blow itself up on top of us? Not on your life. Forget it. All I know right now is that I'm god damned tired. How about a drink?"

No response from Clare who was staring out the window and seemed to be searching the sky.

Adam stepped to her side.

"I can't see it Clare, but maybe there is something out there taking in all of this nonsense. You're a right-minded enough girl, and the religious kind that's supposed to be rewarded. How about you making some kind of a mark with Him and putting in a good word for me? Chances are that's as close as I'll ever come to it. What do you say? We got a deal?"

"Shut up, Adam. And like I said, from here on in let me just wonder what's on your so-called mind."

"Okay. Guess."

"I give up."

"Well I was reading that when the planets finally run out of steam and start back in their reverse course, there are now some guys who think that a lot, but by no means all of them, will collide. The one we're on may be lucky enough to slip on by and escape destruction. And you know, by that time, with interstellar computers and induced high energy fields in deep space, we may just be lucky enough to nudge our way around the universe for quite awhile. And there's even a theory that the planets are speeding up because of dark matter pushing them apart and never will collide. So no more big bangs."

"But what happens when the sun runs out of steam?"

"I dunno. Watch TV. Maybe they'll come up with something on the late night news."

"Adam, knock it off. The problem's always been that you don't love life, at least not the way I do. Here's where it's at, if you haven't noticed. And God, how I love it. Now then, if you don't mind, I'll have a martini... with a twist, if you please."